The Group - Week Four
M. D. MEYER

MISSY

Copyright © 2012 by M. D. Meyer

All rights reserved. Neither this publication nor any part of this publication may be reproduced or transmitted in any form or by any means, electronic or mechanical, including photocopying, recording or any information storage and retrieval system, without permission in writing from the author.

This is a work of fiction. Names, characters, places and incidents either are the product of the author's imagination or are used fictitiously, and any resemblance to actual persons, living or dead, businesses, companies, events, or locales is entirely coincidental.

Unless otherwise indicated, all Scripture quotations are taken from the Holy Bible, New Life Version. Copyright © 1969, 1976, 1978, 1983, 1986, 1992, 1997. Used by permission of Christian Literature International, P.O. Box 777, Canby, OR 97013.

Scripture quotations marked (KJV) are taken from the Holy Bible, King James Version.

ISBN: 978-1-77069-469-9

Printed in Canada

Word Alive Press
131 Cordite Road, Winnipeg, MB R3W 1S1
www.wordalivepress.ca

Library and Archives Canada Cataloguing in Publication

Meyer, M. D. (Mary Dorene), 1957-

    Missy / M.D. Meyer.

(The group ; week 4)

ISBN 978-1-77069-469-9

    I. Title. II. Series: Meyer, M. D. (Mary Dorene), 1957- . Group ; week 4.

PS8626.E933M58 2012   C813'.6   C2012-900664-5

Confront the Abuser

Many well-meaning Christian people advise victims of abuse to skip this step. Somehow, it doesn't seem right to "confront" someone about their sin.

What often happens, instead, is that the victim of abuse is expected to "forgive" the abuser without any public or even private acknowledgement of wrongdoing.

When the confession of wrongdoing is skipped, it makes light of the offense. There is no need for an explanation, an investigation, recompense or conviction in a court of law. The perpetrator need do nothing at all! The burden is on the victim to forgive the sin that has not yet even been acknowledged!

"Away with the noise of your songs!

I will not listen to the music of your harps.

But let justice roll on like a river,

Righteousness like a never-failing stream!"

—the Lord, whose name is God Almighty
(Amos 5:13, 24, 27b KJV)

Your Words

Shards of twisted steel
That tore at my flesh
Opening half-healed wounds

I closed my eyes
And bowed my head
And turned away ashamed

It had to be true
Those things you said
You were the one that I loved

You were the one
Who I owed it all to
You who had given so much

I failed in my courses
I failed to make friends
Duty came first, I understood

My husband was lazy
My kids were all bad
I'd never be half as good as you

My dreams and plans
All had their faults
They crumbled to dust at your feet

Words don't break bones
That's what they say
So why do I feel so broken today?

"Watch your talk! No bad words should be coming from your mouth. Say what is good. Your words should help others grow as Christians."
(Ephesians 4:29 NLV)

Chapter 1

As a family, they had always been close, but Missy had been especially close to her father. Being completely blind since the day of her birth had presented her with many challenges, but it had been her father who had given her the gift of courage, who had cleared the obstacles from her path, and encouraged her to run in joy and freedom.

Always a tower of strength to her, it came as a shock to Missy when, following her mother's death, he had become severely depressed and then addicted to mood-altering drugs. Formerly a prominent neonatal surgeon, her father had first lost his job, then his home and finally his freedom, when in desperation, he began stealing the drugs he needed to support his habit.

The judge, aware of Dr. Peters's history, had sentenced him to a treatment facility rather than giving him a prison sentence.

That had been only three short weeks ago. And already he was coming out for a weekend pass, flying in from Winnipeg to their small northern community of Rabbit Lake.

Missy stared down at the email. He would have to stay with her and Joshua, of course. Missy's sister, Jasmine, had twin babies that were less than a month old. Born premature, they needed a lot of extra care and their household was a busy one.

And they certainly couldn't say that they didn't have room for him here at Goldrock Lodge. The former tourist camp had three upstairs bedrooms and one on the main floor, not to mention the cabins on the property.

But Missy didn't know if she could cope with anything else at the moment. She was just so *tired* all the time! Usually a bubbly, energetic person, morning sickness had sapped her strength while at the same time, a myriad of new responsibilities had been thrust upon her.

It simply hadn't been an option to refuse her brother-in-law's dying request to take care of his daughter, and Cynarra was a spunky little seven-year-old whom Joshua and Missy had immediately fallen in love with.

Besides being pregnant and having an extra little person around, there was also their commitment to restart the youth program as soon as possible. The past winter, the camp had been home to seven troubled teens and as many full- and part-time staff members. It had been a success in many ways but two of their key staff, Michael and Rosalee Peters, had recently resigned, leaving a serious void which had not yet been filled.

And Joshua's poor health was a big factor in their decision as to whether or not they would restart the youth program.

Joshua… Maybe the biggest reason that Missy felt so tired and overwhelmed. In some ways, Joshua had taken the place of her father in Missy's life. After the surgery that had restored her sight, it was Joshua who had helped her through the bewildering new world that she'd found herself in. Being sighted was not as easy to get used to as she had always dreamed that it would be! Joshua had been so patient and gentle with her, giving her the time she needed to get used to things.

And now it was Joshua who needed her. Besides grieving over the recent loss of his brother, Joshua was recovering from a heart attack brought on by overexertion. The doctors were still trying to figure out why, at only twenty-four years of age, Joshua's heart had not been strong enough to handle the strain. There was some speculation that the weakness might have resulted from a childhood illness or possibly an undiagnosed birth defect.

The one person who might know about Joshua's early childhood was in the bedroom with him now. Missy could hear Yvonne Quill's strident voice raised as usual when she was addressing her nephew. Missy couldn't understand the words that Yvonne was speaking in Ojibway, but there was no mistaking the angry, derisive tone.

Missy jumped up from her chair at the computer. She should never have allowed his aunt to visit! The doctor had cautioned Missy that Joshua was to get lots of rest. He wasn't even allowed to climb the stairs. That's why he was in the guest bedroom. He was to do nothing strenuous. No extra worries. No excitement. No stress.

Missy plunged through the bedroom doorway. Joshua was sitting on the edge of the bed, his aunt towering above him. The verbal assault had obviously taken its toll on him. Joshua looked beat down emotionally and physically. His typically well-groomed jet-black hair was looking dull and disheveled and his dark brown eyes were clouded with fatigue. Usually dressed for meeting people at this hour of the day, Joshua was instead wearing an old t-shirt and faded jogging pants.

"Leave him alone!" Missy yelled.

Yvonne stopped the tirade and slowly turned to face Missy, her eyes narrowed and her thin lips compressed into a taut line. Though she had only recently turned sixty, bitterness had gouged deep lines in her face, her black hair was mottled with gray, and her dark brown eyes were perpetually black with anger. Though not especially tall, Yvonne dominated any room she was in, her forceful presence intimidating even the most confident.

Missy returned her glare. "Get out of my house," she said.

"*Your* house!" Yvonne spat the words disdainfully. "I don't think so."

She turned purposefully away from Missy and began to unleash more vitriol on her nephew. Missy, unable to bear any more, advanced toward the older woman. "I told you to leave!" she said angrily, grabbing onto her arm.

Yvonne swore at Missy, including a derogatory label about Missy's African American ancestry, and then she pushed her away, using all the force of her anger. Missy was thrust hard against the corner of the heavy old oak desk.

Pain shot through her body and for an instant, her universe was consumed by it. Then Joshua's arms were around her, his urgent voice in her ear, and only a deep ache remained localized in the center of her back.

Yvonne stood in Missy's line of vision; her chin raised high, her eyes filled with triumphant disdain.

Missy pulled away from Joshua.

"Don't—don't fight her," Joshua pleaded.

Missy turned back in surprise. Did he mean, don't argue with her or did he mean don't physically fight her? "I want her to leave now," Missy said in a trembling voice.

Joshua shook his head wearily and took a step back to sink down into the recliner.

Missy glanced at Yvonne's proud defiance before returning her gaze to Joshua's lowered eyes and slumped shoulders. "Joshua…" she entreated him.

He looked up at her and said in a solemn voice, "She is my aunt."

And that was the end of it! They'd had this discussion before and always it ended the same way. Yvonne was his aunt and could do as she pleased—even if it meant destroying her nephew's life!

Missy strode out of the room, thought she heard a low chuckle and almost dove back into the room again. Controlling her emotions with some difficulty, she walked through the kitchen out into the main part of the lodge. There she hesitated. She didn't want to give Yvonne opportunity to taunt her again. If she went to sit in one of the easy chairs by the fire, chances were that the older woman would follow her, so Missy decided to go upstairs and check out the room where her father would be staying.

She had the choice of two spiral staircases, one on the north end of the lodge and one on the south. She walked purposefully across the expanse of the large dining hall to the south end of the lodge. Maybe she would sit by the fire anyway. No, she should check on the room upstairs…

The late afternoon sun shone in from the skylights above and slanted in from the cathedral style windows that faced the back bedrooms built above the kitchen, garage and downstairs bedroom. Missy opened the curtains of the inside window, wishing not for the first time that there was a window in this room that opened directly to the outside. But Goldrock Lodge had been built flush against the rock outcropping from which it had derived its name. There were outside windows in the other two bedrooms, one facing north and one south.

Missy turned back the cover off the bed—and remembered, with a feeling of dismay that the fresh sheets were downstairs. She would have to go through the kitchen again to reach the laundry area where they were stored. And risk meeting Yvonne again.

Perhaps she would make the bed later, no hurry… No! She had promised herself that she would not let the woman intimidate her. This was her home and she should not and could not alter her plans every time Yvonne decided to drop over.

Still Missy's heart beat a little faster as she tried to walk nonchalantly down the stairs and through the kitchen. If Yvonne was still in the bedroom, fine. If she wasn't there, that was fine too.

She resisted the urge to stop in to see how Joshua was, quickly gathered the sheets and went upstairs again. She started to make the bed and realized that she had gotten a single set instead of a double. If she hadn't been in such a hurry… Yvonne had intimidated her after all! Or had Missy done it to herself?

Angrily, she tore off the sheets, folded them sloppily and headed toward the stairs again. The front door was just closing. Missy could see Yvonne striding past the tall front windows of the lodge, and watched in dismay as Yvonne grabbed her grandnephew's ear and pulled him away from his one-on-one basketball game with Cynarra.

Although Keiron was the same age as Cynarra he was thinner, his hair was scruffy and his clothes were ill-fitting and worn. He wasn't even wearing a jacket!

Cynarra was dressed for the cool spring weather with rubber boots, jeans and a bright pink wind-breaker. A matching hat covered some of the curly black hair framing her lovely dark skin, and accentuated her warm, brown eyes. Missy felt a swell of gratitude for this unexpected little gift from God.

Cynarra looked sad as she watched Keiron being led away but after a moment, she turned and began bouncing the ball again.

Missy went into the laundry room to put the sheets away but didn't take out another set. Fatigue crushed down upon her. The sheets could wait. Her father wasn't coming until the next afternoon, at the earliest.

Suddenly, she heard the front door open again. *Great! Probably Yvonne back for another round!*

"Anybody home?" a cheerful voice called.

Grandma! Missy sighed in relief.

A moment later, her grandmother appeared in the doorway. Though ten years older than Yvonne, the two women could easily pass for the same age. Martha's short salt and pepper hair was naturally curly, framing a round, pleasant face with laugh-lines around her eyes and mouth.

"Hey, baby girl, how're ya doing?" Martha asked in her soft southern accent.

Missy smiled wearily. *What was there to answer to that?* "I'm okay."

"Well, you don't have to worry about making supper, anyhow," Martha said cheerily. "I was making a lasagna for Jasmine and the crew there, and I thought it was just as easy to make two of them."

"Thanks, Grandma." Missy smiled in genuine gratitude. Lately, it had seemed an effort to make any kind of meal at all.

"Where do you want this?" a deeper voice asked.

Missy looked past her grandma to see Charles Kakegamic carrying a towel-wrapped parcel that was quite likely the lasagna, hot from the oven.

Charles, the same age as Martha, had kept his slim build and dark black hair. He was the calmest, most easy-going person Missy had ever known, able to defuse any situation with his slow smile and gentle words.

Missy grinned. "Hi, Charles."

Martha waved her hand toward the kitchen counter. "Over here would be fine," she said, setting her purse and a shopping bag filled with groceries down beside it. "I have the fixings for a salad, too, honey," she said to Missy. "And some garlic bread and some ice cream for dessert. I'll just put that in the freezer…"

Charles, a resident of Rabbit Lake, and a long-time close friend of the family, made himself at home, putting a kettle on to make tea. "How's Joshua?" he asked.

"Okay, I guess," Missy said.

Charles raised an eyebrow and headed straight for the downstairs bedroom, which was off the kitchen. When the place had originally been built as a tourist camp some thirty years before, it had been Martha and her husband's room. Martha had done most of the cooking and Tom had risen early to go out fishing with the tourists.

"You look like somethin' the cat drug in."

Joshua grinned wryly as Charles pulled up the desk chair and sat across from him. "Thanks."

The older man gazed past Joshua at the closed blinds of the patio door. "Saw your aunt on our way over," he said.

The brief moment of levity was gone. Joshua felt as if someone had turned the lights off in the room.

As if in response, Charles suddenly stood up, drew the blinds and pulled open the patio door. He took off his jacket and handed it to Joshua. "C'mon," he said, "some fresh air will do you good."

Joshua hesitated, but Charles's energy was contagious. Joshua put the jacket on over his t-shirt and looked around for his shoes, but Charles was one step ahead of him, arranging the loosely tied runners for Joshua to slip his feet into.

It did feel good to have some fresh air, Joshua acknowledged, as he sank down into one of the wicker patio chairs and Charles took another. The sun was shining, but there was still a thin layer of ice on the lake, making the air chilly but not cold.

Charles continued the conversation as if it had not been interrupted. "She spoke up in council last night. Made some good points."

The words pierced like a knife in his back.

"Not that I agree with what she's trying to do," Charles quickly added. "But she's right about some things."

Joshua remained silent as Charles continued.

"This land originally belonged to our people."

Joshua nodded slightly. He couldn't disagree with that.

"The mineral rights should never have been surrendered."

Yes, but they were.

"The land should have been leased, not sold."

Right again.

"And old man Farrington probably shouldn't have sold this land after the gold was mined out."

Now he was hitting a bit closer to home. The land had been sold to Tom.

From where Joshua sat, he could see some of the old mine buildings and the huge headframe still standing etched against the sky. He hadn't wanted this responsibility. He'd wanted to continue to work beside Tom; not alone without him. It had come as a shock when Tom's will was read and all of his land and most of his money had gone to Joshua.

MISSY

"Some are saying that Tom had no right to give the land and the money to you—"

"The money was his to give!" Joshua interrupted.

Charles sighed. "I know. I've helped him with his books all these years. He put way more into this community than he ever took out."

"Most of his money was made long before he ever came up here," Joshua continued defensively. "And he invested it and it made more money for him. He had somebody really good advising him."

Charles nodded. "Yeah, me," he said sardonically.

Joshua hadn't known that.

Charles shrugged. "Jack of all trades; master of none."

Joshua couldn't keep the admiration from his voice. "You're good at so many things."

Charles shook his head. "I'm a behind-the-scenes man. Tom had all the ideas for the lodge and the facilities for Rachel's Children. I knew how to run a computer program for designing it. Tom had the vision for helping all those babies and then the children's camp and now the youth program. I just did some of the bookwork and told him where to invest his money."

"You did a good job," Joshua commented.

That was an understatement, of course. A wealthy man before, Tom had been exceedingly rich when he died. He'd left a more than adequate annuity for his wife, and his mentally handicapped son, Bobby, was well provided for. The bulk of his money, though, had been left to Joshua. There had been no stipulations and no strings attached—Tom hadn't been that kind of a guy. Joshua had known that Tom wanted him to carry on with their goals for the youth program and he had immediately set out to do that.

Now everything was being questioned: his right to have the money, his ability to run the program, even his ownership of the house he was living in.

Charles stood to his feet. "I shouldn't be laying all this on you. The doc said that you weren't supposed to have any extra stress."

"Too late for that." Joshua forced a grin. "Guess it just seems like everyone's on my case these days."

"Your aunt…"

"Yeah, and the Department of Northern Development and Mines…"

"Now, I told you I was taking care of that," Charles declared. "They said you could have till the end of this summer and it should be no problem. I've been looking into how they 'reclaimed' some of the other mine sites in the area. We can do it."

Joshua was grateful. "Thanks, Charles."

"And I've been working on this other business, too. I've got copies of all the financial records going back the full thirty years that Tom and Martha have been up here."

Joshua stared at him. "Where?" he wondered aloud. Charles' amphibious houseboat, an engineering marvel in itself, couldn't possibly contain so many files, could it?

Charles grinned. "Computer files don't take up so much space." He grew more serious as he added, "I have back-up files in a lawyer's office in Winnipeg."

"Lawyer's office?" Joshua asked weakly.

Charles rested a hand on Joshua's shoulder. "It might get worse before it gets better," he said.

"Do you think…?" Joshua hesitated, searching for the right words. "Do you think we have any chance at all?"

"Of course!" Charles exclaimed, surprise in his voice. "Of course, we have a chance. All I'm saying is that there might be some rough waters up ahead, that's all."

Joshua shook his head. "Don't know if I can handle many more rough waters," he said wearily.

"You'll be fine," Charles assured him.

Joshua wasn't so sure. He turned to look out over the lake. Funny, how everything was so dismal this time of the year, even when the sun was shining. The thin ice on the lake made it appear perpetually gray and the bare trees looked like dark skeletons. On the ground, where the snow had melted, it was muddy slush and only an occasional black raven flew overhead. Officially spring on the calendar, no flowers would appear this far north for at least another month.

Suddenly, a bright spot of color appeared in his line of vision. Joshua smiled. *Cynarra…*

Joshua raised an arm to wave as she ran toward him.

"Daddy!" she exclaimed, running up the steps onto the deck.

Joshua's smile broadened. Cynarra's love was so uncomplicated and freely given. Though his brother had certainly made his mistakes, he had provided the little girl with a father's secure and unconditional love.

Now Cynarra had opened her heart to Joshua, accepting him as an adopted father and calling him, "Daddy."

He leaned forward and opened his arms, and she flew into them.

"You're all better now?" she asked.

Joshua hesitated. Because of her father's death after a lingering illness, Cynarra was overly concerned with Joshua's health. "Well…" he said. "I'm feeling a lot better than yesterday—and tomorrow, I'll feel a lot better than I do today. And the day after, I'll feel even better than I will tomorrow. And the day after the day after…"

Cynarra giggled and a deep chuckle sounded from the other side of the deck. Joshua glanced at Charles, who was regarding him with amusement. "You'd make a great politician," he declared.

"Joshua! Joshua! Where are you?" Missy's anxious cries shattered the tranquil moment.

"We're out here," Charles called.

"What are you doing out here? It's cold. You should have a blanket or…"

Charles put an arm on her shoulder. "He's fine, Missy. We're just getting a little fresh air."

His words didn't seem to be having much of a reassuring effect on Missy. She glanced uncertainly at them, before turning to go with a murmured, "Supper's ready."

Joshua stood to his feet with an effort. Cynarra skipped on ahead of him. "What are we having?"

Missy's voice was still a little subdued. "Grandma made us lasagna."

Charles was the last to come inside, closing the patio door and blinds behind him. Joshua took off his coat and handed it to him with a quiet, "Thanks."

Martha had the table set and the food ready for them. Joshua took a small bite of the hot lasagna but had difficulty swallowing even that much. His throat seemed to be getting worse instead of better. Warm liquids weren't as hard to get down. Thankfully, Charles was setting a cup of hot tea down in front of him.

Suddenly, he realized that he had missed an important part of the conversation. Missy was talking about someone coming to visit. *Her father!* Oh, no, not her father—on top of everything else—and this weekend!

"I can help you get the room ready before I leave," Martha said.

Missy made a noncommittal reply, and changed the subject. "Cynarra, what have you been up to this afternoon? I haven't seen you for a while."

Cynarra smiled. "Keiron and I were playing basketball."

Martha said, "We should have invited Keiron to have supper with us."

Cynarra's smile faded. "His auntie said that he couldn't come up here anymore."

"Now, why would she say a thing like that?" Martha asked.

Cynarra wrinkled her nose, trying to remember exactly what had been said. "He should stay with his own people." She pursed her lips. "But that couldn't be right. We're his people, aren't we? I'm his cousin and you're his uncle, aren't you, Daddy?"

"Yeah, that's right, honey. We're his people."

But even as he spoke the words, Joshua sighed inwardly. Where would it all end? Were he and his family to be completely ostracized from the community? It certainly wasn't Cynarra's fault that there was a dispute over the land ownership.

And it wasn't Keiron's fault, either. With a father in prison and his mother no longer living, Keiron had been raised by his great-aunt Yvonne. Joshua wanted Keiron to feel welcome at the lodge any time he wished to visit.

Martha started talking about how well both the twins were progressing. The conversation swirled around Joshua; the words seemed to be swallowed up into some kind of dense fog before they could reach him. He couldn't think of anything positive to contribute, but everyone else seemed to be talking so maybe he didn't need to say anything at all. He could concentrate all his efforts on trying to eat a little bit more of this lasagna…

Missy's voice sliced through the fog and lifted his spirits. "That was such a good meal, Grandma."

Joshua smiled. Even if he couldn't eat, it was good to see Missy enjoy a meal. She'd had so much morning sickness lately.

Joshua took another sip of tea and smiled reassuringly at Missy. Her answering smile turned quickly into a frown of concern as she noticed that Joshua's plate was still full.

She was about to say something when Charles spoke up. "I've finished a rough copy of the taxes," he said. "Maybe you'd have time to look them over."

"Charles…" Martha's voice was filled with gentle reproof.

"Aw, it won't hurt him to work his brain a bit. We'll go sit by the fire."

Joshua was surprised. The older man was not usually so insistent on things. But Joshua was willing enough to go along with it. He was just thankful that Charles had volunteered his time and his knowledge of computer programs. Muddling through the forms with a pencil and pocket calculator hadn't got Joshua very far and the deadline for the income tax reports was looming.

He followed Charles into the sitting area at the southern end of the lodge. "Think I'll stir up that fire a bit," Charles said as Joshua sank into the big recliner.

Joshua watched as the older man nursed the fire along, strategically adding a log here and there. Joshua put his feet up and leaned back in the chair. Might as well be comfortable; Charles didn't seem in as much of a hurry now.

The flames licked around the logs, rising and falling, glowing bright and then dimming a little, only to flare up once again… Joshua could feel the warmth of the fire now. The sun was going down, adding to the warmth and mellow light as it cast its final glow over the water and through the tall front windows of the lodge.

"It's all printed out," Charles said in a voice that seemed to rise and fall as gently as the flickering light of the fire. "I'll just read it to you; see if I got everything down okay."

Joshua made some small attempt to move. He thought that maybe he should be sitting at a desk or something, but Charles was reading Joshua's name, address, social security number and birth date. And still in that quiet, rhythmic voice: "Now, since you got married this past year, I had to consult the guide…"

In the moment before sleep overtook him, Joshua wondered fleetingly if Charles was perhaps reading more of the guide than he needed to…

Chapter 2

"He's asleep," Charles said in a stage whisper, even though they were well out of earshot of Joshua.

Martha shook her head. "You old fox," she teased. "I thought for a while there that you really were going to work on the taxes with him tonight."

"Nah," Charles waved a hand and grinned. "They're all done."

Missy watching them, wondered, not for the first time, what their relationship was—or was becoming.

"Why don't you go rest, dear," Martha said kindly. "We'll clean up in here. You'll help, too, won't you, Cynarra?"

The little girl grinned. "Yep!"

"All right," Missy conceded. "I am a little tired." She walked over to the sink and opened the cupboard underneath. "The dish-drainer is here…" She pulled it out and put it on top of the counter. "And the soap is here… I think there should be some clean towels in this drawer…"

She felt her grandma's hand rest gently on hers. "I think I know where things are," she said with a smile. "This was my kitchen for almost thirty years, you know."

Missy nodded but in her heart she rebelled. This was *her* kitchen now and had been for several months, and she had also changed things to suit the youth program that they'd been running…

Oh, well, her grandma would discover everything for herself. She must have already looked around a bit since she'd found enough to set the table with.

As Missy turned to leave, Martha said, "Oh, honey, which room did you want me to get ready for your dad?"

"It's okay. I can do it tomorrow," Missy replied.

"No, no," Martha insisted. "It will just take a moment. Are the sheets still where they used to be?"

She was already moving toward the laundry area.

Missy followed her, grimacing as Martha pulled out the carelessly folded sheets that she had put back there.

"Oh, not those ones," Missy said. "Those are single. You'll need a double set."

Martha carefully refolded them as she asked again, "Which room are you planning to use, dear?"

Missy sighed. "I was thinking about our room," she said. "Joshua and I are sleeping down here till the doctor says he's well enough for stairs."

"Cynarra has Bobby's old room?" Martha asked.

Missy nodded. "We had it set up as a nursery when we had the youth program here because some of our girls already had one or two children. But some of Bobby's things are still in the closet and on the top bunk bed."

"I can send them down to him," Martha offered. "I should clear out the other room, too."

"No, it's okay," Missy assured her, knowing Martha was referring to the room she had shared with her husband for as far back as Missy could remember.

Martha smiled sadly at her. "I was actually thinking about giving the bed to Jasmine. When she and Andrew get married, she'll need to replace her single bed."

"Grandma, there's really no rush for you to empty out that room."

Martha smiled tenderly at her. "I'll be pretty busy helping Jasmine with the twins for the next couple of weeks but after that, I'll start sorting through Grandpa's things. And we'll move the rest of Bobby's things out, too."

"So Bobby is going to stay with Coralee and David, then?" The thought saddened Missy even though she'd already guessed that Bobby wouldn't be coming back.

"Yes. He's made some friends and he goes to a day-program down there. Corrie and David seem to like having him and, of course, Alisha and he get along really well."

Yes, Missy could well believe that. Bobby would always enjoy being with children because so many of his interests were still at a child's level. He loved cartoons and simple computer games and he had a child's unending delight in the world around him.

"What about you?" Missy asked.

Martha smiled wanly. "I'm not sure where I belong anymore. It was okay at Corrie's, but it was hard for me to stay… uninvolved. I guess I was mothering everybody too much. Corrie even thought that Bobby should be more independent. That's why she started him in that day program. He does seem to enjoy it." Martha's smile widened. "I know that Jasmine needs me now with the babies. They're quite a handful. It'll be nice when Amy's out of the hospital. Ashley's doing really well, though. She's getting so strong; she can almost hold her head up by herself."

Missy said a little wistfully, "I wish I could go down there and help out more. I've barely seen them since they came home."

Martha patted her arm. "You've had your plate full here, honey. And there's quite a few of us helping already. Jamie and Katie... And of course, Andrew is always there."

"Always?"

Martha grinned. "Well, we do kick him out at night, but he's always back first thing in the morning."

"No, I meant, is he not back at work yet? I thought he was doing better."

Martha reached into the cupboard and selected a pair of double sheets. "Actually, I think he's going to wait and start work later on this summer after things have settled down a bit." She shut the cupboard door. "Amy still has a chest tube in and she isn't gaining weight quite as fast as the doctor's would like. It might be a while yet before she's allowed to come home."

As they continued talking, Missy led the way back into the kitchen. Charles was up to his elbows in dishwater and Cynarra was standing on a chair beside him with a dishtowel in her hands.

Martha laughed. "Oops, I think we came back too soon."

But Charles only smiled good-humoredly. "That's just fine. You two go ahead and have a visit. We're quite capable of doing a few dishes, aren't we, kiddo?"

Cynarra gave them a big grin. "Yep!"

"I put the rest of the lasagna in the fridge for you," Charles added. "Make a good lunch for you and Josh tomorrow."

"I'll go put these sheets on the bed upstairs," Martha said.

Missy smiled her thanks and turned toward the sitting area at the end of the lodge. Joshua was still asleep in the recliner. Missy laid a quilt over him and kissed him lightly on the forehead before sinking down onto the sofa and pulling a quilt over herself as well.

A warm, drowsy, comfortable feeling encompassed her and Missy slept.

WHEN JOSHUA WOKE, IT WAS dark and the fire had gone out. He noticed Missy asleep on the couch and there was a note on the coffee table from Martha: "Cynarra can stay with us, tonight. You kids get some rest! Love, Grandma."

Joshua set the note back down and leaned over to gently shake Missy awake. He said her name and she mumbled something in reply, but her eyes stayed closed and Joshua thought that, if she was sleeping so well, maybe he should just leave her. He took the blanket that he'd been using and added it to the one she had and he turned up the heat as well.

Most of the lights were off, but the kitchen lights were blazing, lighting up the main dining area well enough for him to find his way. Joshua poured himself a glass of water and took a sip. Funny, how sore his throat still was. It even hurt to drink water!

Joshua sighed and set the glass down again. He stepped through the door of the bedroom and stopped as a flood of memories swept over him.

It had been less than a week since his brother had died in this very room.

He'd come, knowing he was dying. And he'd brought his daughter. Bryan's final request had been for Joshua to take care of her.

Cynarra... A week ago, he hadn't even known of her existence. Now the little girl was so firmly entrenched in his heart that she might just as well have been his own flesh and blood daughter.

He'd almost lost her when she'd been attacked by a bear, but he'd arrived in time to scare it away. Then he had carried her out of the bush to safety, walking past the point of exhaustion and talking non-stop to keep her mind off the pain. It had nearly killed him—his heart attack had been brought on by the physical ordeal—but he would do it all over again for Cynarra if he had to.

She was such a spunky little kid. Here it was less than a week after the bear attack and she was already out playing basketball with Keiron. Joshua just hoped that she wouldn't overdo it: Cynarra still had a bandage on her leg where the bear's sharp claws had pierced through skin and muscle. Joshua shuddered inwardly, remembering it all again. So soon after he'd promised Bryan that he would take good care of his daughter.

Well, she was safe enough now with Martha. A retired nurse, Martha would have likely even checked Cynarra's bandage before she went to bed. The two were certainly getting along well. Cynarra hadn't had a grandmother before and she had immediately adopted Martha, calling her Grandma from their first meeting.

With a groan, Joshua walked to the bed and pulled down the covers. Martha had offered to take Cynarra so that he and Missy could get some extra rest. He looked down at the bed. He was tired… so tired. But still he hesitated, feeling grief wash over him once again.

The voice was a comfortable, familiar one, spoken not into his ear but to his heart. "He's not tired any more. You are. Rest now…"

Joshua lay down as the words moved through him and became one with the deep and steady rhythm of each breath. "Rest now… rest now… rest…"

THE RINGING OF THE TELEPHONE pulled Joshua out of a deep and dreamless sleep but was insufficient to motivate him to get up and answer it. He heard it ring two more times before someone answered: in dismay he realized that it was his aunt, and she was speaking in Ojibway. The caller must have thought that it was the wrong number and hung up for that call was cut off, only to be followed by another call less than a minute later. This time, although Yvonne answered in Ojibway, she switched to English. Joshua could hear each word, spoken in quick, impatient tones.

"What? No. He's still sleeping. No, I don't know where she is."

This time the receiver was banged down. Joshua groaned. *He really should get up before the phone rang again.*

Instead he fell back asleep, only to be awakened again by the sound of the ringing phone. This time, he determined to get up and was actually sitting on the edge of the bed when his aunt's voice reached him through the open bedroom doorway.

By the time Joshua had made it out to the kitchen, she'd already hung up.

"Who was it?" he asked.

Yvonne shrugged. "Some woman."

His aunt had made a pot of coffee and Joshua poured himself a cup.

"So your wife finally leave you?"

"What?" Joshua spun around and the coffee sloshed onto his clothes and splashed on the floor.

"She take the kid with her?"

"What are you talking about?" Joshua demanded angrily as he grabbed a dishcloth and wiped at his shirt.

Yvonne seemed amused. "Comes as a shock, does it?"

Joshua hurried out of the kitchen. *Missy had been asleep on the couch. If she wasn't there, she'd gone for a walk or something. There was probably a note...*

He hadn't realized he was out of breath and trembling until he saw her lying there, peacefully sleeping where he'd left her the night before. He forced himself to be calm, to breathe slowly and to relax.

By the time he was back in the kitchen, he was able to speak in a quiet normal voice to his aunt. "Missy's asleep on the couch."

"You two aren't even sleeping together anymore?"

"Of course we are!"

"Doesn't look like it," Yvonne said with a grin.

Joshua knew there was no point to arguing.

"And you thought she'd gone," Yvonne said slyly.

"No, I didn't!"

But he had! In that one wild, crazy moment, he had actually imagined that Missy had left him!

"She'll leave you. One of these days, you'll come back to an empty house." Yvonne nodded her head sagely. "Yeah, she'll be gone."

There was no point in arguing with her. Joshua remained silent.

"So where's my niece?"

Joshua refilled his coffee cup and sat down at the table. "Cynarra stayed with Missy's grandmother last night."

Yvonne's eyes narrowed. "Her own family not good enough for you?"

"Martha is her family," Joshua said. "When the adoption is finalized, Cynarra will legally be Missy's daughter and Martha is Missy's grandmother."

"*Adopted* grandmother, you mean."

It was true. Missy also was an adopted child.

Yvonne curled her lip in disgust. "Too many adoptions these days. Kids should stay with their own families."

"I am Cynarra's family."

Yvonne didn't reply but stood silently to her feet and walked away, leaving him with the hollow echo of his words still in the air and a new worry on his mind. *Would his aunt try to fight him for custody of Cynarra?*

The phone rang yet again, interrupting his thoughts. Joshua sighed and stood to his feet.

He'd been speaking to his aunt in Ojibway and his mind was still preoccupied with Cynarra and Missy. The woman on the phone spoke in a quick, energetic voice and for a moment, Joshua almost thought she might be a telemarketer. Then he started to take in what she was saying.

She was a writer, interested in doing a story about Rachel's Children. She wanted to speak to Tom Peters and Joshua had to tell her that he had passed away almost nine months ago. Then she wanted to know if there was any chance of getting in touch with his son, Jeff Peters. She said that she'd been trying at his last known address but that he had obviously moved…

Afterwards, Joshua thought maybe he shouldn't have been so free with the information but at the time, he just thought the words out loud. "He'll be here tomorrow. Maybe I could let him know you're wanting to get in touch with him."

The woman sounded pleased and excited. "Actually, I'm flying up today. I should be there in an hour or so."

Before Joshua could think of what to reply to that, she had rung off with a hurried, "Oh, there's my call. I don't want to miss the flight! See you in a bit."

Missy came into the room just as Joshua was hanging up the receiver.

"Who was that?" she asked in a sleepy voice.

"Some woman," Joshua said. "She wants to see your dad. She's on her way up here." He looked down at his coffee-stained shirt and headed toward the bedroom. "I'd better change."

Missy followed on his heels. "You want to run that by me again?"

Joshua explained the phone call the best he could.

"But why did you tell a perfect stranger that my dad was coming to visit?"

Joshua shrugged. "I don't know. She was talking so fast. I didn't really have time to think about it, I guess."

Joshua peeled off his shirt and looked around for another. "I don't think I have any clothes down here. Do you think you could grab me some from upstairs?"

Missy frowned and she seemed almost angry as she asked, "A shirt?"

"Umm..." Joshua hesitated. "I was thinking maybe I would take a shower. Could you bring me some pants and..."

But she was already gone.

Joshua shook his head. That was the second woman who had walked out on him today. Not to mention the one who had hung up on him.

Maybe he should just crawl back into bed and start the day all over again! No, he'd better make himself presentable. That woman sounded as if she planned to head straight to the lodge after she arrived.

It was strange that she'd traveled this far and already booked her flight to Rabbit Lake. She was really taking a chance on finding somebody up here that would be able to tell her about Rachel's Children. It'd been so long ago. And now Tom was gone. Martha was here, though. Maybe if this woman showed up, he would invite Martha to come over.

MISSY YANKED CLOTHES OUT AND slammed the dresser drawers shut again. Joshua was so preoccupied with that woman coming that he hadn't even bothered to ask her how she felt. Just assumed that she would do his bidding like a good little wife and go fetch his clothes for him.

Well, she could tell him how she was feeling if he asked. She was feeling lousy! She bent down to pick up the pair of socks that had slipped out of her hand and a wave of nausea swept over her.

She sat down on the bed and caught a glimpse of herself in the mirror. Whoever said that pregnant women had a "special glow" about them must have never seen one in her third month—or her second—or first. People did say that the morning sickness usually ended by the beginning of the fourth month. According to the calendar, that should have been yesterday. Guess the morning sickness didn't just end suddenly. Maybe it would at least taper off soon.

Missy stood to her feet. At least she didn't have too big of a bulge yet. Just enough to look fat instead of pregnant! Even her face seemed puffier. According to the scales, she hadn't gained any weight yet, but her body had definitely rearranged itself!

Missy tried to fix her hair a little but ended up just making it look worse. She needed to give it a good conditioning. But that would require a lot more energy than she had right now. Maybe a scarf… Yes, that looked a bit better. And just a touch of lipstick…

"You look beautiful."

Missy whirled around at the sound of Joshua's voice, then sunk down onto the bed with a groan as the sudden movement caused her to feel sick again.

"You okay?"

Joshua sounded concerned. But when Missy looked up at him and saw him standing there with wet hair and a towel wrapped around his waist, all she could feel was anger. "You're not supposed to climb stairs," she scolded.

"I wasn't sure if you were coming back or not."

"Well, you asked me to get your clothes, didn't you?" she demanded.

"Then you just left… I thought you were going to get me some but then you didn't come back..."

She had taken longer than she'd intended to. But as Missy stood to her feet, a wave of nausea hit her again and, instead of apologizing, she said, "You'd better get dressed up here, in case that woman you invited shows up."

She barely made it down to the bathroom before she threw up. Afterwards she felt weak and shaky. She lay down on the bed and closed her eyes…

It seemed like only a moment later when she heard someone calling. "Hello! Hello—is anyone home?"

Missy struggled off the bed and made her way through the kitchen into the main part of the lodge.

"There was no doorbell. I wasn't sure if I should just walk in…"

The woman, who looked to be in her late thirties, was dressed like a model and had the figure to match. Her flaming red hair looked natural with her milky white skin and green cat's eyes. She smiled sweetly at Missy and asked, "Is this Goldrock Lodge?"

"Yes," Missy replied, looking at the woman's designer luggage with disfavor, "but we run a youth program here, not…"

"Oh, I'm sorry," the woman interrupted, following Missy's eye. "It's just that I was in such a hurry to get here, I didn't bother to drop off my luggage first."

"There's a hotel back down the road that you came in on. You should have turned left instead of right…"

"Yes, I know, dear." The woman stepped forward with her hand outstretched. "I haven't introduced myself yet. My name is Katherine Blake-Jones."

Missy limply shook her hand.

"And you are…?"

"Missy Quill."

"Missy…" She looked at her strangely for a minute, then shook her head slightly and finally smiled brightly again. "I guess there isn't any of the Peters family still living here. But the young man on the phone said that tomorrow—"

"What do you want?" Missy demanded. "Why are you here?"

The woman hesitated. "Perhaps we could sit down?"

Missy gave a fractional nod and they both pulled out chairs at one of the small round dining tables.

"The young man…"

"My husband," Missy stated flatly.

Katherine inclined her head slightly and smiled. "Your husband said that Jeff…"

"My father."

The woman shook her head. "Jeff Peters… He did have a daughter named Missy but she was…"

What?—More beautiful? Better dressed? Not three months pregnant and feeling as if she could throw up every ten minutes?

"She was visually impaired," Katherine finished.

Missy, embarrassed at her wrong assumptions and her unreasonable dislike of the woman, lowered her eyes as she said quietly, "I used to be visually impaired."

"No, dear," Katherine persisted. "I mean, she was totally blind."

Annoyed again, Missy decided to just drop the subject. "So what is it that you wanted to see Jeff Peters about?"

Katherine gazed dreamily around the room. "My father wrote so much about this place—and what has been accomplished here over the years." Her eyes met Missy's again. "He died two months ago and I've been reading through some of his old notes. He was a writer too…" She paused and turned back to Missy. "Maybe you've heard of him—Dylan McPherson."

Missy shook her head. "No, I don't think so."

"Anyway," Katherine continued, "I was thinking maybe I would do one of those stories: *Where are they now?* It's been almost twenty years, but it was quite a sensational story and people might be interested in a bit of an update on some of the babies. And Rachel's Children…" Her eyes glowed a little as she looked around again.

"Can we still go underground? Is any of it still intact? I always wanted to come up here, but it just never worked out. I've seen all the pictures…"

Missy stood to her feet and folded her arms. "It's all been blocked off. Some of the equipment had to be left down there. Most of it was donated to the Rabbit Lake Health Center. There's nothing left to see."

With a faint smile, Katherine stood gracefully to her feet. A ray of sunshine coming in through the skylight lit up her hair, setting it aglow. Curly like Missy's, it was beautifully styled with some of it pinned up and some of it hanging loosely about her smooth ivory face.

Suddenly, she looked upwards and Missy, following her gaze, groaned inwardly. *Joshua...*

Katherine walked across the room to the spiral staircase as Joshua walked down. They met at the bottom and Katherine already had her hand outstretched, ready to introduce herself.

Missy eyed them critically. Joshua was yawning and had a bit of a tousled look; he must have fallen asleep as well. But he, unlike Missy, was no longer dressed in an old t-shirt and sweatpants and he, unlike Missy, could wake up looking great. He was smiling and looking his handsome best as he took hold of Katherine's outstretched hand.

Missy turned her back on them both and walked over to the sitting area by the fireplace. Well, the woman was his guest after all. He was the owner of the lodge. He could kick her out—if he wanted to.

Chapter 3

Joshua was surprised when Missy turned and walked away from their guest, but then just about everything Missy did these days surprised him.

Katherine, with a notebook in one hand, and a pen in the other, immediately launched into a series of questions about the past, present, and future of Goldrock Lodge. She seemed interested in everything and everyone.

She took photos of Joshua in different spots in the lodge and one outside with a full view of Goldrock Lodge in the background. She'd wanted one of Missy and him together but Missy had flatly refused to be photographed.

As the interview lengthened, Joshua's throat got sorer. And although it was still early in the day, he felt totally exhausted! Suddenly, he remembered his intention to call Martha. She'd be able to answer Katherine's questions better than him anyways. He hadn't even been born when Rachel's Children had originally started!

Martha came right over, bringing Cynarra with her. Joshua introduced Katherine and soon the two women were chatting away as if they'd known each other for a lifetime instead of just a few minutes!

Cynarra soon grew restless, and wandered away. Joshua waited a bit and then followed, curious to see what she was up to.

He found her over in the sitting area by the TV. The north end of the lodge wasn't used as much in the colder months, but in summer it provided a scenic view of a rock garden and the old road that wound its way east and then down south.

Cynarra was curled up in the corner of the loveseat, totally absorbed in what certainly didn't look like an average seven-year-old's book. Joshua thought at first that he wouldn't disturb her. Then he noticed the tears in her eyes.

"Cynarra…" he said gently.

She looked up at Joshua. "It's one of my daddy's plays."

Joshua's brother had been an actor and being a single father, Cynarra had often gone to the theatres or TV sets with him. She'd begun to read at a young age and even helped him with his lines sometimes!

"He was a really good actor," Cynarra said. "Everybody always clapped for a long time. People will really miss him."

Joshua moved over to the loveseat and put his arm around her. "You too?"

Cynarra only nodded, too overcome for words.

Suddenly, there was a light tapping at the patio door, and they both looked up to see Keiron standing outside.

Cynarra jumped up and ran to open the patio door as Joshua grinned. *Just what the doctor ordered!*

As the children went outside to play, Joshua wandered into the kitchen where Katherine and Martha were still talking. Martha had made coffee, and she offered some to Joshua. "And maybe we should make lunch soon," she said.

The door from the bedroom burst open. "That's not your job; it's mine!"

Everyone went silent and just stared at Missy.

Katherine stood to her feet. "I should be checking into my hotel…"

"We'd like you to stay and join us." The words should have been an invitation, but Missy made them sound like a command.

As Katherine murmured her thanks, the main door of the lodge banged shut, and Joshua, with a clear view through the kitchen doorway and across the dining hall, saw his Aunt Yvonne striding towards them.

As if with a built-in homing device, she zeroed in on Joshua, and before even reaching the kitchen, was demanding in a loud voice to know whose suitcases were by the door.

Then her eyes were sweeping past him and Missy and Martha to fasten critically upon Katherine. Her lip curled in disdain before she snorted in disgust and turned to face her nephew again.

"You're so rich now, you need two wives?"

Missy's cry of outrage was closely followed by a gentle chide from Martha, "Now, Yvonne…"

Katherine simply stood to her feet, stretched out her hand, and said with a smile, "I don't believe we've met. My name is Katherine Blake-Jones. I'm a freelance journalist…"

"Oh, a journalist?" Yvonne's manner changed immediately. She smiled and shook Katherine's hand. "What story are you working on?"

Before Katherine could answer, Missy interrupted. "I'd like to get lunch ready," she said. "Maybe you could take your discussion elsewhere."

As Joshua led the way out of the kitchen, he felt the need to explain to Katherine that this wasn't how Missy usually treated people. "She's pregnant," he said when they were safely out of earshot. "She has morning sickness a lot."

Katherine smiled understandingly. "That can be very difficult."

Yvonne, overhearing them, spoke to Joshua in Ojibway. "Should've married a Native woman. They don't bother their husbands with such things."

Joshua felt the sting of her words but didn't respond to them.

After they were all seated around the great stone fireplace at the south end of the lodge, Katherine immediately launched into questions, directing her first one at Yvonne. "Have you lived here in Rabbit Lake all your life?"

Yvonne stuck out her chin. "Of course! My people have always been here."

"So you could tell me some of the history of this place," Katherine continued smoothly. "There used to be a gold mine here…"

Joshua groaned inwardly as he slumped further back in his chair. *Of all the people to ask….*

"This land has *always* belonged to the people of Rabbit Lake—the Waboose clan," Yvonne declared. "Back in the 40's some white guy 'discovers' gold and stakes a claim. According to the Indian Act, he only has to pay 25 cents an acre 'rent' at the beginning, four cents an acre while he's developing the mine and 8 cents an acre afterwards. He of course, also 'claimed' the mineral rights underneath the Reserve and has to only pay 5% royalties on what he makes to the Ministry of Indian Affairs and Northern Development."

"Our community benefited a lot from that mine," Joshua dared to interrupt. "Just about everybody was employed there in one way or the other and we all profited. We had hydro and water and sewer before a lot of other northern communities did. Our houses, schools, and community and health centers were made of good materials shipped in on the all-season road."

"Yeah, and where's that road now?" Yvonne demanded.

Joshua didn't answer. Katherine had been taking notes. She looked up questioningly first at Joshua and then Yvonne.

"Hydro-electric plant," Yvonne spit the words out as if they were poison. "They put a big dam up and flooded our traditional hunting grounds so rich white people two hundred miles from here could watch TV and run their electric dishwashers."

"And that also flooded the road that the mine had built?" Katherine asked.

"There were actually two stages of flooding." Martha spoke up for the first time. "The building of the dam officially closed the road, but we built a detour that made it passable during our Rachel's Children years. Not too many people knew we were using it. We still had the tourist camp as a front for our operations and we always flew people in or brought them by boat or snowmobile. In the intervening years, beavers have built dams in various spots using the culverts and roadbed to their advantage."

Katherine turned the conversation back to Yvonne. "So, when the road was flooded…"

Yvonne lifted her chin higher. "It didn't make any difference to my people. We've always traveled by water."

Joshua sighed. "A lot of people fly out, too. I don't know that the closing of the road had that much effect on our community. A lot of people didn't even have vehicles back when the road was still passable."

"You know so much," Yvonne sneered. "You weren't even born then!"

Joshua didn't like arguing with his aunt in front of a guest. He lowered his voice and said in Ojibway. "I learned the history of our people—and of this land."

"From them!" Yvonne pursed her lips toward Martha.

"Also from Grandpa Pipe and old Maggie Keesick," Joshua continued in low tones.

"Both dead."

"And Charles—"

"Joshua…" Martha interjected in a gentle voice.

Joshua suddenly realized that he'd left both Martha and Katherine out of the conversation. "I'm sorry," he said. "Did you have other questions, Ms. Blake-Jones?"

"Oh, please call me Katherine." She smiled. "Actually, I was wondering if I could have a bit of a tour? I know a lot of the buildings are boarded up and the mine has been closed off…"

"I can show you around," Martha offered. She took Katherine's arm and led her across the lodge to the north end of the building, Joshua and Yvonne following in their wake.

Martha pointed through the patio doors toward the old road that led into the bush. "It used to be a lot wider," she said. "It's grown in over the years. People still use it some, for hunting and it makes a good skidoo trail in the winter.

"The garage is over there." Martha pointed through the patio doors and off to her right toward the back of the building. "Our team would drive the van in through the garage and down into the mine—"

Katherine interrupted excitedly, "Is it true that you had access to the mine right from the inside of the lodge?"

"Yes," Martha replied. "Actually, there's three ways to get into the garage and from there into the mine. There's an outside entrance; you could go through the kitchen or…" She paused for dramatic effect. "Let's say someone saw you heading toward that bedroom…" Martha pointed up to the room that had been hers and Tom's for many years. "They wouldn't know about the steps that go down into the garage from there."

"Oh, could you show me?" Katherine asked eagerly, her camera poised and ready.

Martha started up the spiral staircase at the north end of the lodge, Katherine and Yvonne following close behind her.

Joshua stared grimly up at them. It wouldn't have been his first choice to show his aunt all around the place. She already seemed to be taking too much of a proprietorial interest in the lodge.

He was even more concerned after he made his way past Missy who had her back towards him, through into the garage where he found Martha quoting aloud the code to open the door to the decline.

"Everything still work?" she asked brightly when she noticed Joshua.

Martha didn't wait for an answer but opened the door to the control panel and keyed in the numbers.

There was a low whirring sound, and the entire east wall lifted, revealing a dark chasm that seemed to swallow up the bright garage lights.

Katherine snapped picture after picture, and Yvonne peered curiously into the decline.

"What's going on here?"

Missy's voice, coming suddenly from behind, startled them all. Martha responded defensively to Missy's aggrieved tone: "Katherine asked if she could have a bit of a tour while we were waiting. Surely there's no harm in that."

Missy muttered, "Should've charged admission," and went back up the stairs to the kitchen.

Joshua sank wearily down on the steps as Martha continued her role as tour guide. "The decline was already here, of course."

"Decline?" Katherine queried.

"That's a surface entrance to the mine. Trucks would drive in there. It only goes to the fifth level on the north side of the shaft, but that was as far as we needed to go."

Katherine was furiously scribbling in her notebook again. "So your operations were located on the fifth level. How far down is that?"

"About seven hundred feet."

"Could we go a little further in?" Katherine asked.

"There really isn't much more to see," Joshua said. "It's just a big black hole in the ground."

"It looked like a cave of sorts," Katherine persisted.

"Enough rock was blasted away to make an opening big enough for the large mining vehicles that used to travel through it," Martha explained. "The decline is like a tunnel that angles down into what used to be the mine. The mine itself is all flooded now. It naturally fills in with water unless it's being regularly pumped out."

"Which it isn't anymore…" Katherine prompted.

"No," Martha confirmed. "That all stopped when we closed off the mine. We kept a couple of levels of the mine open for people to tour through for a year or two after Rachel's Children was dismantled, but it was quite costly and there was always the risk of someone getting hurt. When we began the children's camps here, we boarded up all the buildings and sealed off all the shafts and mine entrances."

"Except for this one," Katherine noted.

"We talked about sealing this up permanently too," Martha said, "for safety reasons. But in the meantime we keep it locked, and since it's inside our house it's not readily accessible to others."

"It should be sealed off," Joshua agreed. "It's one of the things that we've talked about doing and never got around to, I guess. It's easy to forget it's here. Actually, I'm surprised that the mechanism still works; we haven't had it open in years."

"Lunch!" Missy called out, and Martha hit the switch to close the door to the decline.

Yvonne muttered something unintelligible and pushed past the two women to go out the small side door of the garage.

Katherine tucked her camera away in her bag, but kept her notebook and pen in her hand as she followed Martha and Joshua into the kitchen.

"I've set a table for you out there," Missy said, waving a hand toward the dining hall.

Martha and Katherine immediately resumed their conversation as they took their seats at a table set for seven.

Joshua continued on toward the front door of the lodge to call Cynarra for lunch. He strongly doubted that Yvonne and Keiron would still be there.

Sure enough the two of them were already gone.

Cynarra was sitting on the steps with the basketball in her hand, sadly watching Yvonne and Keiron walking away from them.

"Lunch is ready," Joshua said gently.

Cynarra looked up at him. "She's so mean to Keiron."

Joshua didn't know how to respond. There was no way he could defend Yvonne's actions, but he felt quite incapable of saying anything negative about her either.

"We should—uh—go eat lunch now."

Joshua turned quickly to avoid seeing the confusion in Cynarra's eyes as he led the way back into the lodge.

The table conversation was kept lively by Katherine's questions, and Missy seemed to have regained some of her usual hospitableness as she served soup and passed around the sandwiches that she had prepared.

Katherine asked Martha how Rachel's Children had first begun.

Martha smiled and got a far-away look in her eye. "Hmm," she said, "I haven't thought about that question for quite a while. I guess it really all began with my son… Jeff. He was, in some ways, I suppose, the first of our 'Rachel's Children'."

Katherine looked confused. "I thought that Jeff was one of your doctors?"

"Yes, he was," Martha confirmed. "But when I think back to how it all really began, I'd have to say that it was with that one little baby."

Martha's eyes grew misty as she continued. "Tom and I had only been married for about two years. We were expecting our first child. Tom was still playing college basketball at that time. I'd been working as a nurse in pediatrics for about a year when suddenly one day I was informed that I had been transferred to obstetrics."

"You sound as if you didn't have a choice about that," Katherine said.

"Actually, I didn't," Martha replied. "Back in those days nurses didn't have as much say about their career path as they do today. And I was enough of a rarity back then, being an African-American nurse—I was mistaken for a cleaning lady more times than I care to remember—that I didn't want to draw even more attention to myself by protesting against the establishment. And I did love helping out delivering babies. What I didn't like was having to help out with the abortions that were starting to become more and more frequent."

"What's an abortion, Grandma?" Cynarra asked.

Missy stood quickly to her feet. "C'mon, Cynarra, you can help me get dessert ready for everyone. We're going to have 'Broken Glass'."

Cynarra's eyes grew wide. "What's that?" she exclaimed.

Missy was already on her way to the kitchen, and Cynarra hurried after her. "It has three kinds of Jell-O…"

"Coo-ool!"

Martha said in a hushed voice, "I'll try to hurry through the rest of my story before they get back."

"You were telling us about Jeff…" Katherine prompted.

"Yes. As you may have guessed, Jeff's birth was the result of a late term abortion that went wrong… very wrong."

"Or very right," Katherine said grimly.

"Yes." Martha smiled warmly toward her. "Yes, it was very right and Jeff was no mistake or accident. God knew all along that he would be born." She hesitated, her smile fading. "It was just such a difficult situation and I was still so young and unsure of myself… and I guess what I did was against the law. Legally he was dead but as we were disposing of him I heard a faint little cry. It… it broke my heart. There was just nothing else I could do."

"What—what did you do?" Katherine asked.

"I just wrapped that little baby in my coat and took him on home."

"But the legal implications…!"

Martha grinned. "Yeah, there were those." She shook her head and sighed. "It took us years to get everything all straightened out and by that time we were deeply in debt from all those lawyer fees.

And of course I no longer had my job… and my little baby girl had been born shortly after Jeff came into our lives, so we had two little ones to feed and clothe."

"How ever did you manage?" Katherine asked.

"My Tom was good at a lot of things…" Martha paused to smile at Missy and Cynarra as they walked toward the table, Cynarra proudly carrying a glass bowl that looked almost too heavy for her. "One thing that he was very, very good at was basketball. That same year that Jeff came into our lives, Tom was in the first round draft from his college team. He was voted M.V.P. for three years running during which time his team won the NBA championships. Even after Tom injured his knee, he got a job coaching right away and… well, money was never a big problem after he turned professional."

Missy began to serve up bowls of Broken Glass as Katherine prompted Martha: "And a lot of that money was used to build Rachel's Children?"

"What's Rachel's Children, Grandma?" Cynarra asked.

Martha smiled at her. "It was an organization that helped save a lot of babies' lives. Someday, when you're older, I'll tell you all about it."

As Cynarra opened her mouth to ask another question, Martha forestalled her by changing the subject. "This dessert is very good. I don't think I've ever had it before."

"It's really easy to make," Missy said. "I made the three different kinds of Jell-O yesterday. Last night when I woke up and couldn't get back to sleep, I decided I might as well make use of my time so I put the rest of it together then. The graham wafer crust—"

But Joshua didn't hear any more. One question burned in his mind, blocking out all other thoughts: if Missy had been awake in the night and had gotten up, why had she chosen to go back to sleep on the couch rather than joining him in their bed?

Chapter 4

"Still having trouble with your throat?" Martha asked.

Everyone turned to look at him and Joshua nodded quickly, a little embarrassed by the focus on his health again. And he especially didn't like to talk about it around Cynarra. He looked into her worried eyes and smiled brightly as he scooped up a big spoonful of Jell-O. "This is actually helping my throat to feel better," he declared, popping the spoonful into his mouth.

But Cynarra wasn't buying it. "Jell-O doesn't make you better," she said scornfully. "Medicine does. You should see a doctor!"

"I have a checkup on Monday; I'll be sure to mention it to the doctor then." He grinned affectionately at Cynarra and motioned toward the bowl in front of her. "Eat your Broken Glass," he ordered.

Cynarra giggled and scraped up the last of her dessert.

Joshua heard a faint tapping and looked past her toward the sound. Keiron again!

As Joshua waved him in, Cynarra jumped to her feet. "We had broken glass for lunch!" she cheerfully proclaimed. "And, when my daddy swallowed some of the broken glass, it made his throat feel better!" Cynarra threw a quick smile over her shoulder at Joshua before scampering through the door behind Keiron, giggling all the way.

Joshua exchanged smiles with Katherine who was in his line of vision. He followed the children's progress, watching through the tall windows at the front of the lodge then stood to his feet as they walked down the hill towards the lake. He walked over to the front of the lodge to better see them. They were picking up rocks and throwing them through the thin ice remaining at the edge of the shoreline. With their small lithe bodies and dark hair, they could, from a distance, almost be twins. Closer up, you could tell that Cynarra's mother had been from the Caribbean and Keiron's mother Caucasian. But both were his brothers' children and both held a special place in Joshua's heart.

At the sound of raised voices, Joshua turned quickly back toward the kitchen where the conflict seemed to be centered. He walked in just as Missy was pulling a drying towel out of Martha's hands. "You didn't even ask if I wanted any help. You just took over—like you always do!"

"Oh, baby girl…" Martha said compassionately.

"I'm not your baby girl anymore!" Missy screamed. "And it's not your house anymore. It's not Yvonne's house. And—" She whirled to face Katherine. "It's certainly not yours!"

Katherine slowly set down the stack of dirty plates she'd been holding.

Joshua couldn't believe it. He'd seen Missy angry before but not like this!

He backed nervously out of the kitchen, feeling as if anything he might try to do would just make things worse.

Katherine strode past him, her composure for once, completely shattered.

Martha followed in her wake, tears streaming down her cheeks.

Joshua went after them, thinking he might apologize on Missy's behalf.

Martha was too quick for him, hurrying out the door before he could speak a word, but Katherine was slowed down by her luggage.

"I could give you a ride," Joshua offered as she slung the last of her bags over her shoulder.

"Thank you," Katherine said, a fragile smile appearing on her lips.

As he drove them down the road, Joshua wondered where to begin. He needed to apologize…

Katherine seemed to sense his discomfort, and said, "The first trimester is usually the worst—unless of course you count those last few days when you feel like an elephant and you just want to get it all over with!"

Joshua was grateful for her graciousness, and grabbed at the subject that she had offered to him. "Do you have children as well, then?" he asked.

"Yes," Katherine said with a warm smile. "A son. He's just about the age of your daughter. Here, I have a picture of him…" She reached into her bag, pulled out her wallet and tilted the clear plastic cover toward him. "He's with his Grandma. I didn't want to take him out of school for this trip."

Joshua glanced at the little boy with curly, red hair and a mass of freckles. "Cute kid."

He turned the van into the hotel parking lot, and led Katherine inside to introduce her to the hotel manager, Mike Williams.

As Katherine foraged in her bag to retrieve her credit card, Mike bent toward Joshua and said softly, "Sorry to hear about your brother."

Joshua nodded in acknowledgement. "He's with the Lord now."

A surge of joy filled Joshua's heart as he said the words: it was true. His brother was free from all pain now. *Home-free...*

"Is there a coffee-shop here?" Katherine's voice broke into his reverie.

"The best in town," Mike answered. "Betty just pulled a pie out of the oven. I'll get you both a piece. You go on in there and I'll take your bags to your room for you, Miss."

Joshua shook his head, but Mike wasn't about to take no for an answer. "Look, it's on the house. I gotta get down on my knees and beg you or what?"

"Actually, Joshua, I was hoping you could tell me a bit more about the mine—and about Rachel's Children," Katherine prompted.

"Martha's really the one you should be asking..."

"Now, don't stand out here in the hallway. There's a fresh pot of coffee. Just help yourself," Mike said, as he picked up Katherine's bags.

"And don't worry," he added. "If Missy calls, I'll just tell her you're on a hot date with a beautiful redhead."

"Mike!" Joshua felt like decking him, but the older man was already halfway down the hallway, laughing as he went.

"He was joking," Joshua said angrily.

Katherine looked at him strangely. "I know," she said.

Joshua felt like kicking himself. She knew. He knew. Everyone knew. It was just a joke. Mike was always talking like that. It was just his way.

Still, he should get back to the lodge.

But Katherine was already heading towards the coffee pot, and Betty was hurrying across the room toward them with two slices of her special "mile high" lemon meringue pie.

Knowing when to accept defeat, Joshua sat down with Katherine, and prepared himself to answer more of her questions.

But for once, she had information to give instead. "I remember all the excitement when the Rachel's Children story broke. I was just finishing high school and hadn't decided what career to choose yet. I think it was that story that decided things for me."

Joshua thought that Katherine looked a lot younger than she was if she'd been in high school twenty years ago...

"We really didn't know which way public opinion would go," Katherine continued enthusiastically. "I suppose everyone up here, Martha and Tom, and Jeff included, could have all been arrested. What they were doing was certainly illegal."

"Illegal—but not wrong," Joshua interjected. How could it be wrong that so many babies had lived instead of died? Missy had been one of the babies deemed worthy of death. Sarah, the wife of Rabbit Lake's Chief of Police, had also been one of Rachel's Children. And there were hundreds of others...

Katherine agreed. "Sometimes things aren't as clearly right or wrong as they seem at first. A lot of the decisions people make are based on what the media presents to them."

"You're saying most people don't know how to think for themselves?"

"No," Katherine replied, "I think people are just really busy with their lives and don't take the time to search for the truth and to get all the facts in both sides of the argument. And we can't all be experts on every topic. I believe that's the role of the reporter."

"But you do have to pick a 'side' yourself, don't you?"

"Maybe eventually. I think every reporter does slant their story somewhat. But at the beginning, at least, it's important to keep an open mind, if you can."

"If you can...?"

Katherine shrugged. "It's not really a big deal. There'll always be someone who reports from the other perspective. It's better that way. People can read both sides of an argument and judge for themselves. That's democracy. If we ever just start presenting one side of a story..."

"But isn't that what your father and Jenny did?"

"There were others who presented the opposite view. So, again, both sides were presented to the public. But who could deny the right of those little babies to live? No one who saw Missy could look at that beautiful little girl and say that she should have been aborted instead." Katherine smiled. "I think truth was definitely on our side that time."

"Sometimes the answers aren't so easy," Joshua said.

"For example...?"

"The land that old Mr. Farrington sold to Tom thirty-odd years ago, and that Tom then willed to me this past year: did Mr. Farrington have a right to sell it? Did Tom have a right to give it to me? Do I have a right to keep it? And if I die, who should the land go to?"

Katherine leaned back in her chair. "So, do you actually have a deed for this property?" she asked.

"Yes, everything was in order legally. The money too... There was a lot of money..."

"And if something were to happen to you?"

"That's part of the problem. Normally, it would just go to my wife. But my aunt believes that I should make a will so that, if I die, all the land gets transferred back to the original owners—I mean *the* original owners."

Betty came by at that moment to refill their coffee cups. "But neither of you have tried a bite of my pie!" she exclaimed.

Joshua apologized. "My throat's a little sore," he said. It was an understatement. His throat was *very* sore, and he needed to get home and lie down soon.

Katherine smiled up at the waitress. "I promise to eat it all," she said. "It looks wonderful. How ever do you get the meringue to fluff up so high?"

Betty leaned towards her and whispered, "I actually sneak in a couple of extra egg whites."

Katherine laughed. "Never thought to do that!"

Joshua handed Betty his untouched piece of pie. "Maybe you could box it up for me, and I could bring it back for Missy."

"Oh, didn't you see her?" Betty asked. "She was just here a few minutes ago."

"She was?"

"Yeah, her and Cynarra. She's such a cute little kid. I thought they might be joining you two. But then they just left. I didn't even get a chance to talk with them."

Joshua stood quickly to his feet. "I'd better go."

"What about the pie?"

Joshua didn't take time to answer her. All he could think about was Missy.

HE DROVE QUICKLY BACK TO the lodge, hurried inside, and called out Missy's name. Receiving no answer, Joshua looked all around for her. He paused at the bottom of the stairs; he'd already been up there once against his doctor's advice. He stood back a ways and could see that all the bedroom doors in the upstairs loft were open. Surely, she would hear him if she was up there. He called her name tentatively and then louder and louder as a kind of desperation seized him. "Missy! Missy!"

The sound of his voice seemed to echo off the high cathedral ceiling, a hollow mockery of his deepest fears.

His aunt's words echoed through his mind.

She'll leave you. One of these days, you'll come back to an empty house. She'll be gone.

She'll be gone... she'll be gone...

"No!" Joshua gasped. "No! She's upstairs asleep or she's out for a walk or she went to see her sister. She's not gone. *She's not gone!*"

Joshua hurried quickly to the phone, dialing Jasmine's number with trembling fingers.

She wasn't at her sister's and she wasn't at the other five places Joshua tried, growing more desperate with each phone call. He tried the hotel and got a snide remark from Mike. He called the Health Center and was rebuffed by a busy nurse.

A plane flew overhead—the afternoon flight out of Rabbit Lake.

Joshua dropped the phone and stared through the high front windows until the plane was just a dark speck in the sky. Then it was gone, too.

Despair swept over him as Joshua desperately searched for some other explanation. Missy wouldn't just leave! Sure, things were a bit difficult lately. But she wouldn't just leave him without a word.

She'd come to the restaurant... And left without speaking to him.

Joshua wished he could turn back the clock. He should have called Katherine a taxi. He shouldn't have had coffee with her. Missy had been moody all day; she probably hadn't been feeling well. He should have stayed with her. Made her some of that herbal tea she liked…

She couldn't be gone!

Joshua turned toward the spiral staircase at the south end of the lodge. It was closest to the bedroom that Cynarra was using. Missy wouldn't have taken her without her clothes. Cynarra wouldn't have gone without her beloved books.

Joshua started up the stairs, going slowly at first and then hurrying faster and faster as panic rose in his throat and he called her name once again.

"Missy…" His throat was dry, his voice was hoarse. "Missy… Cynarra…" His chest hurt, but he pushed himself onward. He had to know.

He let go of the railing and stumbled across to the open doorway.

They'd packed in a hurry.

Clothes hung out of open drawers and were scattered on the bed and floor. Only one of her suitcases was gone. Cynarra must have taken only what was most important to her.

Joshua sank to his knees. His head was spinning. He felt as if he was going to be sick. And the pain in his chest was almost unbearable now.

Everything grew hazy.

One thought remained clear.

He should have made his will after all…

Chapter 5

THE DARKNESS WAS FAMILIAR AND terrifying to Missy.

Her worst fear had been realized—she was blind again!

She blinked her eyes frantically, in denial. No! No, it couldn't be! It wasn't fair to lose her eyesight twice in one lifetime! It wasn't fair. It couldn't be true...

No—it had to be a dream! Please, God, make it all a dream! Don't panic, she told herself. *Try and think!*

Her head hurt. And she was lying on her back, on something hard. Maybe she'd fallen and injured her head, and that's why she couldn't see. Her injury had affected her eyesight somehow...

Wait! Had she lost her hearing too? It was never this quiet. There was always a bit of noise—the hum of the fridge, a clock ticking... Now, there was nothing. Nothing at all.

Maybe it really was a nightmare. If she couldn't move.

She raised one hand a little, and then higher... she could move! She felt such intense relief that she laughed out loud. It sounded strange and too loud in the absolute stillness around her. Okay — not a nightmare. Not deaf. And not buried alive.

It was the silence that had put that thought into her mind. And the darkness. And the air... so cold and damp.

The ground beneath her... She was conscious enough now to realize that it was rock; not as smooth as cement, nor resilient like wood.

She tried to push herself up to a sitting position. Her head spun; nausea swept over her, her arm gave out from under her and Missy sank back down into oblivion.

JOSHUA KNEW HE WAS ALIVE. For one thing, his head hurt. And his right arm was numb. A sure sign of life, he thought wryly.

He pushed up on his left hand and rolled over a bit so that he could free his right arm. His head was pressed up against the bedpost; that probably explained the headache.

He spied a pillow that had fallen off the unmade bed. He thought it might be within reach, if he could pull himself over just a bit and stretch his left arm out.

It took all his strength but as Joshua laid his aching head down on the cushiony softness, he knew it had been worth it.

He'd sleep for just a bit. Then, when he woke up, he'd think about the things he needed to think about.

MISSY OPENED HER EYES FOR a second time and for a second time, felt terror clamp its cold, steel manacles around her body.

The cold remained, but the fear gradually subsided. She might be blind, but she might also just be somewhere very dark and very quiet.

And not a grave... Somewhere large... A cave... A tunnel...

It came to her slowly and the thought brought relief rather than renewed panic. She was in the mine, probably the decline.

Someone would find her. Someone would come for her.

Missy tried to sit up again. This time she moved more slowly and succeeded in raising her head without passing out. She pulled her legs up and wrapped her arms around them. She was marginally warmer in the huddled position and she rested her head on her knees, allowing herself a few minutes before trying to move again.

She couldn't remember how she'd gotten here.

Missy tried to think of what she could remember.

Katherine... Yes, she remembered her. Perfect, perfect Katherine.

Casual elegance... That's what they'd probably label her style in a magazine ad. Bet she'd never had a bad hair day in her life! Bet she'd never been pregnant either.

Missy felt a tear trickle down her cheek. It had hurt to see Joshua laughing and talking with that woman. *Well, he could have her!*

But Missy knew in her heart that she wasn't being fair to Joshua. He was always polite to guests. It was just who he was. And, more than that, it was part of his job as owner and director of Goldrock Lodge.

And he'd never looked at another woman. Ever since they'd met when they were just teens, he'd only been interested in her—and she in him. He'd never flirted with other women or even joked about it, as some men did.

Missy had to admit that she was just plain jealous.

Jealous of Katherine's vitality and cheerful disposition and casual good looks. Things that had once defined Missy herself. Now all she felt was sick and tired all day, every day.

Had she driven Joshua away? Joshua... so faithful and loving. But perhaps even he had a limit to his patience.

Maybe she'd pushed him away. And Katherine had been there, waiting.

Missy shook herself mentally. She was just making herself feel worse.

And there were more pressing concerns—like survival.

She had to figure out where she was and then try to find a way out. If it was the decline...

Missy moved slowly so that she wouldn't get dizzy again. She didn't feel strong enough to stand, but her jeans were made of heavy material, so she decided to try crawling until she hit something solid. Then once she'd found one wall, she'd move around it until she came to a door or opening of some sort.

Having a plan gave her new courage and Missy set out optimistically in what she hoped was a straight direction.

She fully expected to reach a rock wall. When instead, her hand touched cold, hard metal, she cried out in fear and scuttled back a few feet.

She'd been so sure that she was in the decline. Now, she was back to having no idea at all.

Maybe she was blind after all. And she wasn't in the decline. Maybe there were people close by who could hear her.

"Hello..." Missy said in a tentative voice. "Is someone there? Hello?"

Her words were swallowed up whole by the dark silence.

Panic suddenly gripped her and Missy began to tremble uncontrollably. Now she was shouting the words, "Hello! Somebody! Anybody!"

The shouts turned to screams. "Help me! Somebody help me!"

The silence remained unmoved, untouched by her pain. Dizzy and nauseated, Missy crumpled forward, her sobs gradually diminishing as she drifted back into unconsciousness.

Joshua woke suddenly, feeling as if there was something urgent that he needed to do. *Missy... Missy!*

Joshua groaned and rolled over on his back, remembering everything in an instant. Cynarra was gone. Missy was gone.

Tears ran down his cheeks, trickling into his ears. Joshua tried to brush them away, but they were coming too fast. He rolled over onto his side, his knees drawn up, and his arms wrapped tightly around his chest as if to keep intact what each huge racking sob threatened to tear apart.

Afterwards, he didn't know if he had passed out or simply fallen asleep. He became gradually aware of darkness around him and a deep emptiness within him. He felt totally drained of all energy and emotion.

The darkness was lit a little by the stars that shone faintly through the window. Their twinkling light did nothing to cheer him. Missy wouldn't have stayed away all night if she was coming back. She wouldn't have stayed over at her sister's all night without telling him. She wouldn't have taken Cynarra...

There were no more tears; just a cold, empty, silence.

Joshua became vaguely aware that he was shivering and reached up to pull the duvet off Cynarra's bed. He hadn't moved too far from the pillow. He pulled it under his head, pulled the duvet up around his shoulders, and once again fell into an exhausted and dreamless sleep.

MISSY PULLED HERSELF UP FROM the depths of sleep—or unconsciousness—and once again opened her eyes to a dark, cold world.

She felt drained, emotionally and physically; her body limp and her mind stalled. She had no ambition any longer to explore her surroundings. Someone would find her—or they wouldn't.

She might die before they found her. She was thirsty. How long could a person live without water? How long had it been? There was no way to measure time without light. When she'd been blind, she'd had an electronic watch that spoke the time aloud at the press of a button. The watch she had on now was a simple one with hands that turned. She'd been so proud and happy to have a "regular" watch like everyone else. Now, she'd give anything for her old one.

Impossible to tell how long she'd slept or been unconscious. This was the third time she'd awakened. Likely hours then. She was thirsty; she needed to go to the bathroom and she felt sick to her stomach. The nausea might be from hunger, but it also might be from her head injury or even from the pregnancy.

Her baby… She couldn't bear the thought of him dying.

"Oh, God, help me!" she prayed. "Help my little baby…"

Was it possible that the child had already suffered some harm? She couldn't go without water for long. She'd have to find some—if there was any to find. For her baby's sake.

Cautiously, she lifted her head a little. Maybe if she moved slowly… Her arms felt weak but able to support her weight as she raised herself to her knees. She crawled forward, reaching out as she had before.

Missy recoiled instantly at the touch of cold metal. Then she willed herself to reach out again; move her hand along. Some of it was flaky, likely old and rusty. The metal stopped. Missy shifted her position along a little further and willed her hand to keep moving. Something softer now but a little rough. And rounded. A tire! It had to be!

With renewed energy, Missy pulled herself up higher, reaching, touching... A door! She grabbed onto the handle, heard a satisfying creak of metal and reaching inside, felt the seat, the steering wheel. A car— an old car. Or a truck... There was an old truck in the decline. They'd just left it there. It was too old and rusty to be bothered with.

No light had come on when she'd opened the door. The battery would have died many years before. Missy climbed up into the driver's seat, pulled the creaky old door shut and placed her hands on the steering wheel.

It was such a relief to have something normal, something familiar, around her that Missy began to weep. Her heart swelled with gratitude. "Thank you," she whispered, resting her head on the steering wheel, as the tears continued to fall.

After a few moments, Missy began to move around again, reaching her hand out along the dashboard, feeling beside her and around her. She was definitely on a bench seat and there was a window behind her. For sure a truck then, and almost for sure, located in the decline.

Time and space: as necessary for human beings as food and water.

She was pretty sure that she knew where she was. And she had a rough idea of at least the date. It had to be late Friday night or early Saturday morning. If she could only remember what had happened...

There had been someone yelling... angry words... directed toward Missy. But she couldn't go beyond that. When she tried, the memories seemed to recede further away and everything got jumbled in her mind.

The need to empty her bladder finally drove Missy out of the safety of the truck. She walked unsteadily, feeling the sides of the truck and remembering how it was parked in the decline. If she walked straight back from it... about ten steps...

Missy kept her hands stretched out in front of her. Ten steps... Eleven...

She put aside the rising feeling of panic. She'd stepped out into the unknown. Could she even find the truck again?

Twelve... Her fingers contacted the rough, rock wall. Missy gasping and laughing with relief, ran her hand along the wall, hurrying now. If she moved to the right...

It was there! The door to the decline!

There was a switch up on the wall, similar to the one in the garage.

All she had to do was flip the switch and she was free!

Missy felt her way past the huge wooden door until she encountered rock wall again. The switch was in a open metal box with rough, rusted edges.

With trembling fingers, Missy pushed the switch.

It didn't move!

She pushed harder and harder, frantically jamming down on it with the heel of her hand. It still didn't move!

The awful realization finally hit home as Missy slid despairingly down onto the rock floor. The switch was old... rusty and broken down like the truck.

Maybe if it had been enclosed in a box like the one in the garage... Maybe if it weren't so damp with the mineshaft filled now with water...

She reminded herself that someone had successfully opened the door just today—or was it yesterday? In any case, it had been opened once and it could be done again. It would be again! Missy just needed to be patient. Joshua would miss her. Joshua would look for her. It was just a matter of time. Just a matter of time...

CYNARRA HAD NEVER KNOWN A night so long. Usually a good sleeper, she had lain awake through all of the sounds of creaking floors and doors opening and shutting. Finally, the house had grown silent as everyone else slept.

Cynarra felt fear and something close to despair.

She didn't know what time it was. She had no way of measuring the moments and hours that she lay on the hard, lumpy mattress. And the adults in her life had, once again, been replaced.

Her leg hurt. The doctor had warned her that she shouldn't run around too much. He'd been right.

It hurt inside her tummy, too. She hadn't been able to eat the tough bits of meat in the salty soup that had grease floating on top of it. Even the noodles in the soup had a strange taste and Cynarra had swallowed down a few because she was ordered to, not because she wanted to. Now she was hungry, as that woman had said she would be.

Tears rolled down her cheeks, wetting the thin pillow beneath her head, but Cynarra was careful to not make any sound. She'd gotten a slap across the back of the head for crying at the supper table. Crying wasn't allowed. Neither was laughter. Keiron had gotten a slap for that. He'd made a joke about the moose meat in the soup, saying it was probably from an old cow. He'd been trying to cheer Cynarra up but it hadn't worked anyway and it had bothered her a lot to see him get hit, more than it had bothered her when she herself had been hit.

Cynarra was glad at least that Keiron was here with her. He was a good friend. But he wasn't her mommy or her daddy.

JOSHUA WOKE UP WITH A raging thirst. Carefully he pushed himself up on his feet, and shuffled to the bathroom. Water from the faucet would have to do for now—he was so weak that there was no way he could make it all the way downstairs to the kitchen.

But he didn't want to go back to the bedroom—the thought of going back in there was just too much, to see Cynarra's things scattered about, to know he had lost her…

Missy must have packed in an awful hurry to have left such a mess behind. She must have been really angry!

Joshua sank down against the outside wall of the bedrooms. He could see through the rails over the main part of the lodge. Most of the objects were still deep in shadow, but the darkest part of the night was over. It would soon be dawn. Through the high front windows of the lodge, Joshua could just make out the dark gray mass of the lake. It had been a clear night. Maybe it would be a warm sunny day and the rest of the ice would melt. Joshua shivered. He should have grabbed the duvet from Cynarra's room but he didn't have the energy anymore to move now.

At least he was facing the front door. He could see anyone who came in. Maybe Missy would come back today. Maybe she would come back this morning…

STEPPING OFF THE PLANE AND walking into the Rabbit Lake airport terminal gave Jeff Peters a strange feeling, as if he'd wandered onto a film set and the cameras kept rolling, inadvertently making him a part of the story.

He'd been here before and played so many other parts, but this time he had no idea what role he was expected to play, if any.

During the Rachel's Children days, acting as a neonatal surgeon, he'd been a hero of sorts, being instrumental in saving the lives of many premature infants.

After the demise of Rachel's Children, he'd been gone offstage for many years, and then had returned a broken man, keeping in the background, letting the play unfold around him.

Now, would he be regarded as a villain? In the past three weeks he hoped that he had fully faced who he was and what he had done. Would his family and friends be able to forgive him and accept him into the community again? Or would he remain an "extra" on the set…?

"Good morning, Dr. Peters," a friendly voice called out.

Jeff smiled wryly as the ticket agent strode toward him. Old Pete was definitely a "regular" in the cast of players at Rabbit Lake.

"You're looking great!" Pete exclaimed, pumping Jeff's hand in greeting. "It's good to have you back."

"Thanks." Jeff felt a surge of gratitude. If everyone else was as warm and friendly as Pete…

Jeff looked around. "Missy's not here," he said.

"She's probably on her way," Pete reassured him. "Here, come around and use my phone if you like."

Jeff hesitated. He knew Missy had a lot on her plate right now with Joshua just out of the hospital and their niece living with them now as well. But he couldn't stay with Jasmine. Not after what he'd done… the misery he had caused.

"Maybe—maybe I'll just wait for a bit," Jeff said hesitantly. He found a chair facing the runway, picked up an old dog-eared magazine, and absently began to thumb through it.

Pete hovered nearby. "You sure?" he asked.

"Yeah, I'll just wait."

Jeff tried to focus on the words in front of him, but his mind was elsewhere. *Maybe he shouldn't have come back yet. Maybe it was too soon.*

"Jeff!"

His mom... He hadn't seen her since his arrest, but the love in her voice was as generous and unconditional as ever. Jeff grinned wryly. *Thank God for moms.*

But as he stood and turned toward her, he saw she was not alone. *Jamie... and her son, Andrew!*

Jeff closed his eyes momentarily. *If Andrew had died...*

But he hadn't. Jeff looked at the boy and saw, reflected in his eyes, the sorrow and regret that he himself felt. And Jeff remembered that Andrew had been the arresting officer.

Jeff quickly closed the distance between them, his hand outstretched in greeting. Andrew took his hand and Jeff drew him into a hug.

Andrew's responding embrace said all that needed to be said between them. They drew apart and Jeff asked, "How are you feeling?"

"I'm fine," Andrew said. "It's Amy. She's not doing so well. Will you help us—please?"

Jeff's heart skipped a beat. *Amy—one of his granddaughters!* He hadn't even met either one of them yet. And now to hear that Amy wasn't doing so well...

He grabbed up his bag and started firing questions at Jamie as they hurried towards the door, certain that she, as a nurse, would be able to give him some idea of what the current problem was.

But Jamie just shook her head. "We don't know what's wrong. Her oxygen levels are down. The doctor was going to medevac her out; then we heard that you were coming. It was like an answer to prayer, Jeff."

They were waiting for him at the Health Center, Dr. Smith, looking relieved and grateful, and two young nurses ready to assist as needed.

But for an instant, when he first saw his tiny granddaughter, Jeff was totally incapacitated. His heart was in his throat as he touched her cheek and gently spoke her name. Never could he have anticipated or even imagined this great outpouring of love that he would feel towards a child that was not his own.

Jamie spoke his name in an urgent whisper, and suddenly Jeff was a doctor again. Though he still knew on one level that this was his granddaughter, Jeff was able to detach himself enough to ignore her fragile cry as he pricked her tiny heel to get a blood sample. And for the next two hours, he continued to concentrate on detaching himself emotionally enough to function as the highly qualified neonatal surgeon that he was.

He'd had a lot of practice the previous year working on autopilot. Many times he had been called in to advise on cases, and even in his deepest depression and drug-induced lassitude, he'd been able to function well as a doctor.

It was as a human being that he had been unable to function, his heart frozen up solid with grief. Now, he felt open and vulnerable, and after keeping his emotions under tight control for over two hours, Jeff rested his head on his granddaughter's Isolette incubator and freely wept.

Jamie had hurried out to update Andrew, knowing he would in turn call Jasmine, who was home with the other twin.

Jeff stayed around for a bit longer before he left Amy in Dr. Smith's care, letting the young doctor know that he could call at any time if he had any concerns at all.

Both Jamie and Martha decided to stay with baby Amy. Andrew offered Jeff a ride, which he gladly accepted. He was reluctant to leave his one granddaughter, but anxious to meet the other.

But as Andrew opened the door of the house, and ushered him in, Jeff once again felt as if he was in the wrong script or had been demoted from a major to a minor part in the play.

He'd built the house for his bride, Jenny. Now, their daughter, Jasmine, was welcoming him as a guest and assuring him that he could stay overnight if he wanted to!

During the past winter, he had lived here as a ghost, isolated from the living by a thick, dark fog of depression.

Now as he hugged Jasmine, he felt new life coursing through his veins. "How are you doing?" he asked as he gently released her.

"I'm fine," Jasmine said. "And I'm just so glad you were there to help Amy. Andrew said that she was so much better. They won't have to send her out now, will they?"

"No, honey," he assured her. "I think Amy will be fine now. We had to put her chest tube back in again—give her little lungs a bit more time to develop."

"Yes, Andrew explained it to me," Jasmine said. Tears filled her eyes as she gazed up at him. "And Andrew said you were better, too. Are you?"

Jeff nodded. "I'm drug-free," he assured her. "There's some really good counselors at the treatment center. And…" He hesitated, unsure how to describe the spiritual healing he'd been experiencing. "I guess you could say that… God and I are talking again."

Jasmine smiled through her tears and said, "Me too."

Jeff gave her another hug, feeling a deep joy settling into his heart.

He thought he couldn't possibly be happier. Then he saw Andrew coming towards him with a tiny bundle in his arms.

"And this is Ashley," Jasmine said proudly.

Jeff took the little girl in his arms and kissed her, breathing in the scent of new life and hope. Her eyes fixed on his and she smiled up at him.

"She smiled at me!" Jeff exclaimed.

Jasmine laughed. "It's only a gas bubble, Dad. The nurses at the hospital told me that babies can't smile until they're two months old."

Jeff felt let down for all of about two seconds then he grinned down at his granddaughter and whispered, "We know better, don't we, princess?" And she smiled up at him again!

Gas bubbles… right!

"Can you stay for lunch, Dad?" Jasmine asked.

"Sure can!" Jeff replied.

Andrew put his arm around Jasmine. "Do you need help, sweetheart?"

"That'd be nice," Jasmine replied, gazing lovingly up into his eyes.

As they kissed each other, Jeff couldn't help but smile. It was so good to see his daughter happy again. "So you two gonna get hitched soon?" he asked.

They quickly drew apart and Andrew said, "Uh—yes, sir."

Jeff, realizing that their relationship was still too fragile to bear teasing, spoke with deep sincerity. "It will be an honor to have you as my son-in-law. I look forward to getting to know you better."

"Uh—thank you, sir."

Jeff raised an eyebrow. Must be Andrew's RCMP training. "Just Jeff will do," he said lightly. "Or Mr. Peters if you prefer. I guess you could even call me Dad after the wedding if you want to."

Andrew and Jasmine grinned at each other and Jeff, watching them, felt a well of gratitude rising up within him. Things could have turned out so differently!

Jasmine and Andrew began to discuss lunch preparations together, and Jeff strolled contentedly out of the kitchen into the living room area.

He was surprised to find a woman there. She was just rising from the sofa. She turned towards him and Jeff stopped and stared in wonder. Her beauty and grace took his breath away! She smiled and stretched a hand out in greeting towards him.

Jeff shifted his granddaughter into the crook of his arm and took the woman's hand. "Jeff Peters…" he said by way of introduction.

"Katherine Blake-Jones."

Her voice was as lovely as she was. And her smile…

"I was hoping I would see you… again," she said.

Again? There was something vaguely familiar about her…

"Have we met before?" Jeff asked.

"It's been almost twenty years," Katherine said with a smile, as she gently extricated her hand from his.

"You must have been just a little girl."

Katherine's light, melodic laugh was like a wind chime. "Last year of high school," she said. "But thanks for the compliment."

"I don't remember…" Jeff said. "I should."

Katherine shook her head. "You were looking at someone else at the time." She smiled. "Maybe you remember my father, Dylan McPherson…"

He remembered her now! Dylan McPherson's daughter. She was right; the day they had met, he'd only had eyes for Jenny. But he'd been introduced to Dylan and his wife and their daughter... Katherine.

He eased down on the sofa, keeping Ashley in a comfortable position while he angled his body to face Katherine who sat down again at the other end of the sofa.

The moments flew by as they reminisced about that time so long ago. So much had happened in the intervening years, and Katherine was full of questions for Jeff.

Jasmine interrupted them to announce lunch, and the conversation shifted to talk about babies. Andrew offered to take Ashley from Jeff, but she was sleeping contentedly in his arms.

He was reluctant to let her go even after they had finished lunch. But he was anxious to see his other daughter, Missy, as well. He had been surprised when she hadn't met him at the airport.

Katherine had assured him that she would be staying in the area for a few more days, and reluctantly, Jeff said goodbye to her as well.

He knocked on the door of the lodge, once more feeling like a pseudo-stranger. This place had been his home for so many years.

There was no answer, but the door was unlocked. Jeff opened it a little ways and called out, "Hello!" He stepped inside and closed the door, calling out again, "Hello... Anyone home?"

Jeff's greetings were met with silence. But he had seen both of the lodge vehicles outside... Missy and Joshua had to be around somewhere. Jeff set his bag down at the door and walked around the ground floor of the lodge, continuing to call out as he went.

When he came to the garage, a sudden irrational fear overtook him. He tried to shrug it off, certain that it was his conversation with

Katherine about Rachel's Children that was resurrecting all of the horrible memories of Jenny being trapped in the decline so many years ago.

He felt an overwhelming desire to open the door and release her.

Jenny—his precious Jenny. After all these years, Jeff could still remember the fear and desperation of that moment when he'd found her and thought that she was dead.

No! He wouldn't allow himself to be drawn back into the past. He had lived that way for almost an entire year. He'd come so far. He couldn't— *wouldn't*—give way to grief again.

"God help me!" he prayed.

Jeff gritted his teeth and forced himself to turn away from the door to the decline. *It was twenty years ago!* And Jenny was really and truly dead now.

He noticed a box on the opposite wall that was labeled with his name. Curious, he opened the lid and peeked inside.

Another flood of memories burst forth as Jeff saw that it was collected mementos his mother had packed away for him... his graduation cap, an award from university, his first stethoscope.

Jeff smiled as he closed the lid of the box. He had many good memories from the past—and most of them included Jenny.

He walked resolutely out of the garage, determined to focus on the good memories that he had of the past. And there would be new memories to build in the future. Jeff's thoughts dwelt fondly on his two new granddaughters. Maybe he'd go back over and visit again for a while, at least until Missy and Joshua got back home again.

He looked at his bag still left by the front door, and decided to carry it upstairs. Missy had already told him which room he would be staying in.

He picked up his bag, turned, and for the first time, looked up at the loft of rooms and the walkway in front of them. Jeff's heart skipped a beat as he saw through the railings the inert body of his son-in-law!

Chapter 6

Jeff dropped his bag and raced up the stairs, suddenly fearing the worst. Joshua had just recently survived a heart attack. If Martha hadn't been close at hand and started CPR on him right away...

"Joshua!" Jeff exclaimed, bending anxiously over him, automatically taking his pulse and noting the flushed cheeks and bead of perspiration at his hairline.

Joshua opened glazed eyes and tried to speak but though his dry, chapped lips moved, no sound came from them.

"Wait, don't try to talk yet. I'll get you some water first," Jeff said quickly. He hurried into the bathroom, filled a cup from the faucet, and returned to kneel at Joshua's side.

Holding Joshua's head up a little, Jeff encouraged him to take small sips, until the cup was empty. It was slow going, not helped by the fact that Joshua was shivering violently.

"Joshua, I'm going to get you a blanket... okay?"

Joshua nodded slightly, and Jeff went into the nearest bedroom, returning a moment later with a duvet and pillow.

"Better?" Jeff asked as he tucked the heavy feather duvet close in around Joshua.

Joshua nodded again, but he was still shivering. Jeff touched his forehead. "You're burning up," he said.

He put his fingers on the sides of Joshua's neck. Sure enough, his glands were swollen, indicating some sort of an infection.

"Let me see your throat," Jeff said.

Joshua obligingly opened his mouth and Jeff angled Joshua's head toward the strong afternoon sunshine coming in through the tall front windows.

It was not hard to make a diagnosis. "You have a bad case of strep throat," Jeff said. "How long has your throat been sore?"

"Since the hospital... but they told me it was laryngitis from talking too much." He managed a wry grin. "Plus the ambulance guys stuck a tube down my throat."

Jeff nodded. Certainly, these two events might have made the soft tissues in his throat more susceptible to the Streptococcus bacteria.

"But it kept getting worse instead of better..." Joshua trailed off.

"I'd like to get you started on an antibiotic," Jeff said. "Are you on any other medication?"

Joshua averted his gaze. "I'm supposed to be on heart medication, but..."

"When did you take it last?" Jeff asked urgently.

"Yesterday morning," came the meek reply. "Uh—guess you better get it for me. It's in the bedroom beside the kitchen."

Jeff hurried downstairs to get the pill bottle, remembered his stethoscope in the box in the garage, and grabbed that too, once again shrugging off the crazy feeling of desperation he experienced when close to the decline.

He ran back up the stairs, grateful to the treatment center for their emphasis on good nutrition and exercise. He was feeling more fit than he had in years.

He helped Joshua to take the heart medication, and then listened to his chest, placing the stethoscope in several different spots to get an overall picture of what was happening. Jeff wasn't a cardiologist but had repaired or replaced enough heart valves as a neonatal surgeon to know that this was what likely should have been done for Joshua when he was a baby. It could still be done. Probably at this point, it would be best to completely replace the damaged heart valve.

"Josh…" Jeff said gently.

A faint smile. "Can't seem to keep my eyes open."

"That's okay," Jeff assured him, encouraged that the young man could still smile, if even a little. "Who's your cardiologist?" he asked.

Joshua gave him a name that was familiar to Jeff. He'd worked with Dr. Phillips in the past. "May I call him?" Jeff asked.

Joshua gave a little shrug and another feeble smile. "Sure."

"And I'm going to call in an antibiotic prescription for you as well. But first, let's get you more comfortably situated. Maybe in Bobby's old room—"

"No!" Joshua cried hoarsely, his face contorting in pain.

Jeff stared at him in confusion. "I just thought you might be more comfortable lying on a bed…"

Joshua rolled over onto his side. "She's gone!" he moaned in anguish. "She's gone."

Jeff rested his hand gently on Joshua's shoulder. "Who's gone, son?"

"Cyn…Cynarra—and—and Missy." The words came out in shuddering gasps.

"Where?" Jeff asked in a careful voice. "Where did they go?"

"I don't know!" Joshua cried. He turned his head away again and wept freely. "I don't know."

Missy was gone? And hadn't even let Joshua know where she was going?

"How long ago?" Jeff asked.

"Yesterday..." Joshua drew in a shuddering breath. "Yesterday afternoon."

Jeff rocked back on his heels. He couldn't believe it. He just couldn't believe it!

"There has to be some reasonable explanation," he said, "Missy wouldn't... just leave."

Joshua struggled to raise himself into a sitting position, and Jeff hastened to help him. Once Joshua was sitting leaning against the wall, Jeff tucked the duvet around him again, and sat down beside him.

Joshua stared straight ahead. "She's been unhappy."

"She wouldn't just leave you, Josh—not without an explanation. I know my daughter."

Joshua shook his head. "She's been different lately."

Different? How different could a person become? But Jeff knew the answer to that; he'd experienced huge changes in his own life after his wife had died.

"Why?" Jeff asked. "Why has she been different lately?"

Joshua sighed deeply. "I don't know. Just everything I guess. I know she's been having a lot of morning sickness. My Aunt Yvonne has been coming over more often—and they've been having arguments..."

Jeff shook his head. It still wasn't a good enough explanation for him.

"Aunt Yvonne said that Missy would leave me some day," Joshua spoke sadly. "And she was right."

"No," Jeff said. "She was wrong. Missy wouldn't do that. Not without telling you—or telling anyone else. Jasmine would have said something if she'd known. And I talked to my mom and Jamie. No one said anything. Missy wouldn't have just left without telling anyone!"

But the cold hard fact was: Missy was gone—and Cynarra with her.

Jeff gently squeezed Joshua's shoulder. "I'll be right back, okay. I'm just going to get a phone."

Jeff called the Health Center first. He recognized the nurse who answered the phone—Sarah Hill—and asked her if she'd seen Missy or Cynarra that day. When Sarah replied in the negative, Jeff asked to speak to the doctor who was on duty that day, the same one with whom he had consulted that morning about Amy. Jeff requested a throat swab kit and an antibiotic for Joshua, and asked the doctor to just send them over in a taxi.

Jeff's next phone call was to the house on Sandy Point. Martha answered. "Amy's doing so much better!" she exclaimed. "Jeff, it was so wonderful that you were—"

"Mom…" Jeff interrupted, "Have you seen Missy?"

"No, honey, I haven't."

Jeff noticed that her voice had cooled by several degrees. He hesitated, unsure of how to proceed further.

"We had a bit of a disagreement," his mother spoke into the silence. "She asked me to leave."

Jeff could still think of nothing to say. Missy's relationship with her grandma had always been remarkably good.

"You could ask Joshua," Martha suggested.

"He doesn't know," Jeff said. "He hasn't seen her since yesterday."

"Oh!" Martha exclaimed. "Well, let me ask Jamie. She's here now, too. And Jasmine…"

Jeff waited until his mother came back on the phone. "They haven't seen her for a day or two," she said, a little breathlessly now. "I'll call around. Have you tried the Health Center?"

"Yes," Jeff said, "she wasn't there."

"Okay," Martha said, her voice filled with concern now. "I'll make some phone calls and get back to you. Tell Joshua not to worry. I'm sure she's fine."

Jeff pressed the "off" button on the phone and turned to Joshua. "My mom said to tell you not to worry," he said gently.

The words hung in the stillness of the air, and Jeff suddenly wished that he could retrieve them. Of course Joshua would worry! His wife was missing!

"She's going to phone around," Jeff said. "And she'll call us back as soon as she hears anything."

Joshua still didn't reply but just stared straight ahead.

"I'll fix us some tea," Jeff said, rising to his feet, anxious to be doing something. "You need to get some fluids into you."

Jeff hurried down to the kitchen and made two cups of hot tea with lemon and honey, hoping it would help to soothe Joshua's throat a bit.

As he worked, Jeff kept his back turned purposefully away from the garage—and the decline. Strange, how it kept drawing him…

He was setting the drinks onto a tray when the taxi pulled up with Joshua's prescription. Jeff added Joshua's medicine to the tray and took it up to him.

Joshua was where he had left him, still staring out over the lake.

It reminded Jeff sharply of himself just a few short weeks before.

Jeff set the tray down and knelt beside his son-in-law. "I'm just going to take a throat swab first," he said gently.

Joshua dutifully opened his mouth and a moment later, accepted a dose of the antibiotic.

"Try some of this tea," Jeff suggested next.

Perhaps too weary to protest, Joshua reluctantly took the cup from him, but he did take one sip, quickly followed by another.

Jeff relaxed, leaning back against the wall as they both drank in silence.

Jeff looked out over the lake. "The ice is gone," he said softly.

"Yes," Joshua said.

It was truly beautiful. The lake sparkled in the afternoon sunshine.

The winter was over.

Jeff sat in silence with Joshua for a few minutes before venturing to speak again. "I haven't been a very good support to you and Missy."

Joshua shrugged it off. "It's all right."

"No," Jeff said quietly, more to himself than to anyone else. "No, it wasn't all right. I hurt a lot of people…"

He was silent for a moment, remembering.

"You feel as if you're at the end of your rope and you hold on and hold on. Each day is a struggle, but you hold on because it's the right thing to do and it's what everyone around you expects. Then one day, you just give up. You let go of the rope and you think that, now, life will be easier. No more struggling to meet other people's expectations. Nothing and no one matters anymore.

"Then one morning you wake up and realize that you weren't just in limbo somewhere. You hadn't stepped out of the human race. You were still part of a family. And all the while you thought you were off in another world, you were actually doing damage—major damage—to your family and friends."

"It was like you weren't even here anymore," Joshua said softly.

Jeff turned toward him. "I felt as if I wasn't." He shook his head sorrowfully. "But I was."

Joshua said with something like awe in his voice, "You've changed."

Jeff nodded. "Yeah."

"It helped you then—the treatment program."

Jeff nodded again. "Detox was very hard to go through, but afterwards my mind felt so clear. All the fog was gone and everything was so sharp and focused."

He looked back towards the lake again as he continued. "The pain that I thought I'd left behind was still there, but I realized that I'd rather feel pain than to feel nothing at all. The drugs had acted like an anesthetic to my emotions. I couldn't feel the pain, but I couldn't feel any other emotions either—like joy or love or even anger."

"Anger's a good thing sometimes," Joshua observed.

Jeff turned toward him. "Yes, sometimes." He wondered if it had been his daughter's fiery temper that had gotten them into the mess they were in. He still found it very difficult to believe that she could have left Joshua.

"Whatever you guys are going through…"

Joshua turned away.

"…I'm here for you now. Any way that I can help…"

Silent tears began to trickle down Joshua's cheeks. "Do you think she'll come back?" he whispered hoarsely.

"Yes, I do," Jeff said positively. "Missy's like her grandpa. She gets mad quick and she gets over it quick." Jeff waved toward the front door. "She'll probably walk through that door any minute."

"I hope so," Joshua said in a fragile whisper.

"And I do mean it when I say I want to be here for you guys," Jeff added. "For you and Missy and Jasmine and Andrew and all my grandkids."

That brought a smile as Joshua looked up and said, "It won't be long before you have another one."

"I told Andrew that he could call me 'Dad' if he wanted to," Jeff said. "If you felt comfortable…"

Joshua grinned. "Might take some getting used to but I'll give it a try—Dad."

Jeff smiled back at him. Then he grew thoughtful again. "There's another Father who wants to help you guys…"

Joshua nodded. "Yeah, I know," he said softly.

"I'll pray, if you like," Jeff offered.

Joshua nodded again. "Yeah, I would like that."

Jeff prayed simply, asking their Heavenly Father to watch out for His kids and to bring them all safely back together again. And he prayed for Jasmine and Andrew and their new family and for himself that he could be the father and grandfather that he needed to be.

The phone rang before he even had a chance to say "Amen."

It was on the floor beside him and Jeff answered on the first ring.

The voice on the other end belonged to a child. "Hello," she said tentatively, "Who is this?"

"My name is Jeff Peters," he answered, his mind racing. It might be just a wrong number or it might be Joshua's young niece, Cynarra… "May I ask you what yours is?"

"I don't have very much time," the little girl said. "She just went out for cigarettes. She's going to be back soon."

Not Cynarra then—Missy didn't smoke. But the little girl sounded so anxious that Jeff couldn't just brush her off. "Yes…" he said encouragingly, "how can I help you?"

"You have to tell me who you are first!" the little girl cried urgently. "Is my daddy there? Is Joshua Quill there?"

"Yes, he's here." Jeff said, watching as hope and fear mingled together in Joshua's eyes. "Cynarra, where are you?"

The little girl was sobbing now. "I have to hurry. She's going to come back soon. Please, can you tell my daddy something for me?"

"Yes, I will," Jeff promised.

"Tell him that my mommy is behind a big door. You have to go through our kitchen into a garage."

Jeff almost dropped the phone. He jumped to his feet and was halfway down the stairs when Joshua called out.

Jeff stopped and turned back. "Missy…" His voice shook. "Missy's in the decline." Then he was running down the steps again and speaking into the phone, "Cynarra, honey, tell me where you are."

The little girl said in a tear-filled voice. "She says I have to call her 'Auntie' but she's not my auntie. She's not!"

Another voice, a young boy's, spoke in the background. "Here she comes. Hang up quick!" And the phone clattered down in Jeff's ear.

He dropped the phone on the table as he ran through the kitchen and into the garage. Jeff reached the switchbox and stood still, panic flooding over him. The code number—what was it? It had been so automatic those many years ago.

Jeff closed his eyes and cleared his mind. Then he reached up and quickly keyed it in. The door of the switchbox clicked open and Jeff slammed his hand down on the switch.

As the huge door began to swing open revealing the huge, dark cavern, time seemed to fold in upon itself.

Automatically, Jeff looked at the spot where Jenny had been so many long years before. *Missy wasn't there!*

Jenny wasn't there!

"God help me!" he prayed desperately.

"Missy!" he called in a voice hoarse with emotion. "Missy!"

Jeff turned and frantically scanned the garage shelves for a flashlight. There! He grabbed onto the large 9-volt flashlight and clicked in on.

The old truck! Someone was inside!

Jeff shone the light through. *Missy!*

She was leaning against the door. Jeff opened it carefully and lifted her up into his arms.

Again time seemed to accordion back and forth between the past and present, merging into one meaningless blur.

Jenny… Missy… Jenny…

Jeff focused on the task of getting her out of the decline… into the light… into safety.

He carried her quickly into the house and laid her on the couch, then with trembling hands rushed toward the fireplace. He had to build a fire. She was cold. Jenny was cold.

THE BRIGHT LIGHT HURT HER eyes, but Missy didn't want to shut them. She wanted to gaze forever at her husband's beloved face. She had been so sure that she would never live to see him again.

He looked ill. Missy thought he must have been sick with worry over her.

Tears filled his eyes and his voice shook as he said her name. She tried to answer him, but her throat was too dry.

"You need some water," Joshua said.

No, she didn't want him to leave, not even to get her water. She clung desperately onto him and Joshua said in a gentle voice, "Don't worry. I'll stay right here. Your dad can get you a glass of water."

She watched her father walking slowly toward them. He had the same glazed look in his eye that she remembered from the months after her mother's death. Then suddenly there was a change, and compassion and interest lit up his face as he leaned over her.

"How are you feeling, honey?" he asked.

"Her throat's really dry," Joshua said. "Could you get her a glass of water?"

Her father smiled and said, "Sure. I'll be right back."

As Joshua turned back to face Missy, a myriad of emotions crossed his face. He seemed happy and sad and nervous all at the same time. When he finally spoke, it was in a choked whisper. "I thought you'd left me."

The words took a moment to sink in. Then they hit with all the force of a sledgehammer.

"You—you weren't even looking for me," Missy whispered.

She vividly recalled that in this very room, less than a week before, there had been a major search party organized when Cynarra was found to be missing. But now, when she was missing, he had somehow jumped to the conclusion that she had left him!

Could he think so little of their relationship—their marriage—their love?

He hadn't even been looking for her!

Missy had released her grip on his hands. Now, she drew even further away from him, physically and emotionally.

Her father was back with a glass of water in his hands.

Missy remembered that it had been her father who had found her.

"I'm just going to lift your head up a little," he was saying.

Missy gratefully swallowed down the whole glass of water, trying hard to follow his instructions to sip it slowly.

"Another?" she gasped eagerly.

"We'll wait just a bit. Your body's been deprived of water for quite a while. Since yesterday sometime—"

Her father broke off and glanced questioningly at Joshua.

Joshua bowed his head. "Yesterday afternoon."

He hadn't even been looking for her!

Missy started to cry. She just couldn't help it.

Chapter 7

DEEP, CRIPPLING FATIGUE WEIGHED HEAVY on Joshua's soul. He had failed Missy. Failed her in a way that a husband never should. If he truly loved her, how could he imagine, even for a moment, that she had left him? In retrospect, there hadn't been any real evidence. She had never even threatened to leave him! He jumped to the conclusion because of what…? She had gone missing; that was all.

He should have organized a search party for her as he had just a short week ago for Cynarra…

Cynarra!

He grabbed Jeff's arm. "Cynarra!" he gasped. "Where's Cynarra? You were on the phone with her…"

Jeff shook his head. "I don't know. She didn't say."

"But she knew Missy was in the decline…?"

"Yes, she told me that," Jeff replied hesitantly, "but then she said that she had to go. She sounded afraid of someone who was returning—someone who she said wasn't her aunt…"

Joshua groaned. *His Aunt Yvonne!* It had to be. He should have insisted that Jeff give him the phone. He could have talked to Cynarra.

It had taken all his effort to get down the stairs and then all his thoughts had been consumed by Missy…

Once again, he had failed to protect his brother's child.

"I wonder how Cynarra knew you were in the decline," Jeff said to Missy. "Did she see you get trapped behind there—and try to find someone to help?"

Missy shook her head then winced as if that slight motion hurt. "I can't remember… Someone was shouting… It was a woman…"

"Aunt Yvonne…" Joshua said in a faint whisper.

Missy stared intently at him. "Yes. Yes, it was her. I remember now. She was in the house when Cynarra and I came back… from the restaurant. She had opened the door to the decline… We argued… She hit me… I don't remember anything else after that."

Joshua turned away again, feeling deep shame. His aunt was usually only violent with her mouth but occasionally the verbal abuse did turn into physical abuse. She'd slapped and hit Joshua enough over the years.

But this…! How long would his aunt have left Missy there in the decline? If Missy had died, his aunt would have been guilty of her murder!

"Joshua, do you know where Cynarra is?" Jeff asked. "I can go and get her—"

"Don't go alone!" he warned.

Jeff raised an eyebrow but was forestalled from speaking by a knock on the front door.

"Hello! Is anyone home?" Katherine's cheery voice called out.

Jeff waved his hand. "Over here!"

Katherine's smile faded as she saw Missy and Joshua. Her gaze rested on Jeff. "What happened?" she asked.

He raised his index finger, indicating that he'd answer her in a moment and asked again, "Josh, where is Cynarra?"

"I think… I think she's with my Aunt Yvonne."

Jeff started towards the door.

"She lives—"

Jeff turned back. "I know where she lives," he said, his voice gentle. "Will you two be okay?"

Joshua nodded, but lacked the courage to look at Missy.

Katherine asked, "Do you want me to stay?"

"No, I think it might be better if you came along," Jeff said. Then his voice faltered a little. "Uh, if you don't mind…"

Joshua suddenly remembered that Keiron would be there, too. If Jeff and Katherine succeeded in getting Cynarra away, Yvonne would be very angry and Keiron would be left alone to bear the brunt of that anger. "Keiron… the boy…" he said. "Can you get him too?"

Jeff hesitated and Joshua, anticipating his question, said, "Neither one of us have legal custody of Keiron. His father is in jail; his mother is no longer living. I am his uncle."

Jeff smiled reassuringly. "We'll do what we can," he said.

The silence in the room after they were gone seemed to go on forever.

Joshua couldn't look at Missy.

Another knock on the door!

Joshua looked over and was surprised to see Martha standing hesitantly just inside the door.

"Hello! Anybody home?"

Joshua called, "Over here!" but his voice sounded cracked and hoarse.

As Martha approached, Joshua glanced over at Missy. She had turned toward the back of the couch and had her arm up over her face. Joshua knew she was crying.

Martha didn't see Missy at first. Then, as she came closer, she breathed a sigh of relief. "You found her."

"No... I..." Joshua felt he could not take any credit at all for it.

Missy, with a quick little gasp, turned and raised her arms up. "Grandma!"

Martha's mothering instincts and nurse's training sprang into action. Joshua edged away, feeling worse than useless.

HER GRANDMOTHER TOOK HER HAND and gently smoothed away the strands of hair that clung to Missy's wet face. "Honey child," she said softly and the compassion in her voice brought fresh tears to Missy's eyes.

"Tell me all about it," Martha continued in a soothing voice.

Her throat was still dry and her voice hoarse as Missy replied, "I was in the decline. At first I didn't know where I was. It was so dark and I was scared. I thought maybe I had gone blind again."

Missy noticed a quick movement from Joshua on the periphery of her vision, but kept her eyes focused on her grandmother as she continued, "I couldn't get the door to open. The switch is jammed or something..."

Rare anger flared in her grandmother's eyes. "That entrance to the mine should have been cemented off when the others were. I don't know why no one's bothered to do it yet."

"Grandma," Missy said, "Can you help me walk to the bathroom?"

Compassion flooded the older woman's eyes again. "Of course, child."

With her grandmother's help, Missy had no problem sitting and then standing to her feet. She didn't even feel dizzy as she had expected that she might.

JOSHUA HEARD THE SHOWER RUNNING and a few minutes later Martha bustling about the kitchen, likely getting Missy something to eat.

She was being taken care of, by someone more competent than he.

Joshua sank down into a chair.

He felt cold—shivery cold—but couldn't find the strength to stand up again and get a blanket—or a jacket—or something...

JOSHUA WOKE TO A BUZZ of voices around him. They swarmed like bees, away from him and then near again.

Then he heard his name being called.

Yes?

But they were calling him again, more urgently now. Maybe they hadn't heard. Joshua forced his lips to move.

Yeah...

"He should never have left the hospital, not to come home to *this!*"

Joshua was surprised at the depth of anger in Jeff's voice.

He tried again to speak and must have managed something because Jeff switched to talking directly to him, instead of about him. "Joshua... I'm going to arrange transportation for you to the Health Center."

Joshua gazed up into Jeff's anxious face and managed a feeble, "Okay." Then it was too much effort to keep his eyes open so he closed them.

Voices swam around him again. Jeff was speaking to someone on the phone. Katherine was putting a blanket on him and asking him if he wanted another. Cynarra was asking, "Is Daddy going to die?"

No!

Joshua forced his eyes open. "No," he whispered hoarsely as he sought for, and found, Cynarra's little face, pinched tight with fear. "No," he said with gentle reassurance and even managed a smile that he hoped looked convincing.

Katherine put her arm around the little girl. "Your daddy's going to be okay," she spoke with clear confidence.

Joshua looked past her, saw Keiron and allowed his eyes to close again. The children were safe and Missy was in good hands; that's all that really mattered.

"What's going on here?"

They were wheeling the stretcher in; Jeff was in the middle of taking Joshua's pulse; and he thought the answer to his mother's question could wait for a few seconds.

"We're taking Joshua over to the Health Center," Katherine spoke up.

"What's wrong with him?" Martha asked.

"His heart," Jeff said. "Quite likely mitral stenosis."

"Yes, but..." Martha shook her head. "...He seemed fine yesterday."

"Well, he's not fine today," Jeff said emphatically. "Do you know where Missy is?"

"Asleep hopefully. I did manage to get her to eat a little first..."

"You'll have to wake her up. Tell her..."

"No!" his mother almost gasped the word. "Do you know what kind of an ordeal that poor child has been through in the last two days?"

"Twenty-four hours," Jeff corrected, glancing over at Joshua. They were fixing an oxygen mask over his face. "He appears to have a streptococcal infection in his throat. Besides the obvious current danger, this may offer at least a partial explanation of the heart damage that has already occurred and may still occur in the future."

"Rheumatic fever!" Martha exclaimed.

Jeff nodded. They were starting toward the door now.

Jeff glanced back at the assembled group. The two children looked frightened, especially Cynarra. Katherine edged closer to them and smiled at Jeff. "I'll stay here with them," she said.

Martha turned and stared at the younger woman.

As Jeff hurried after the stretcher, he grinned wryly. They were both strong capable women and intelligent besides. They would surely work out their various caregiving roles. His main concern now was for Joshua.

They'd likely put an IV in and that would be a better way to administer the antibiotic, too. He should have an ECG done STAT. It was too early for results on the throat swab but maybe the lab could give him a preliminary report…

Jeff, with great effort, restrained his thoughts. He wouldn't be the attending physician. He couldn't practice medicine again until after his treatment program was ended. He jumped into the back with Joshua anyway. If he wasn't here as his doctor, he'd be here as his father-in-law. Either way, he'd make sure the boy wasn't abandoned again.

Strange, that was how he felt about him. It wasn't just that his obvious physical needs had not been met, but the young man seemed emotionally neglected as well.

At the Health Center, Dr. Smith readily discussed Joshua's case with Jeff and included him in every decision. Together they made a conference call to Joshua's cardiologist in Thunder Bay.

Dr. Phillips, Jeff's senior by several years and a specialist in heart problems, quickly established himself as the senior member of the team. Dr. Smith communicated the test results to him and the initial procedures that had been done. Dr. Phillips expressed his approval of what they'd done but was dismayed at Joshua's physical condition. He was particularly concerned about the streptococcus infection. He questioned Jeff's assertion that the damaged mitral valve could have been caused by rheumatic fever.

"It's virtually unheard of in developed countries," he argued.

Jeff explained that Joshua had not always had the best of care as an infant and young child. It was possible that he'd been quite sick and no one had bothered to take him in to the Health Center, or the "Nursing Station," as it was then called.

Dr. Phillips said that he was scheduling a balloon valvuloplasty for Joshua but if he thought that the heart valve was badly damaged by rheumatic fever, it might be better to do a complete valve replacement, likely a mechanical prosthesis because of Joshua's young age.

They discussed the options for a few more minutes. Dr. Phillips ordered complete bed rest for Joshua. He made some additional changes in medication and gave some recommendations as far as regular tests and frequent evaluations, but his main concern was for Joshua to have complete rest.

"I'd like a nurse with him at all times," Dr. Phillips continued. "Can you arrange that?"

Jeff made a quick decision. "He'll have a doctor with him at all times."

Dr. Phillips expressed surprise and Jeff explained that he was Joshua's father-in-law, that he was in Rabbit Lake for the weekend, and had no other urgent commitments.

He made a quick call to the lodge. Katherine answered the phone, explaining that Martha was feeding the children an early supper in the kitchen. Missy was still asleep. Katherine said that she would stay as long as she was needed or wanted, and that Charles had arrived at the lodge and was also anxious to help.

Jeff told her that everything was being done for Joshua that could be done and that it was very important for him to have complete rest. Katherine promised to convey the news to everyone else.

Joshua was placed in a sort of suite at the end of the hall that was often used if there was family staying overnight with the patient. There was a separate bedroom, bathroom and a sitting area with a full-sized couch, a table and two chairs.

Joshua was given a sedative and in the dark, quiet, bedroom, quickly fell soundly asleep. He was still on a bit of oxygen through a nasal cannula and had an IV administering fluids, as well as an antibiotic. He was connected to a bedside cardiac monitor, which Jeff regularly checked.

A sign was put on the door, saying "No Visitors Allowed" and Jeff settled in for his long vigil, knowing that for the most part, not a lot would be required of him. The cardiac monitor would continuously send an EKG tracing to the nursing station, and an alarm would sound if Joshua's heart rate went significantly above or below normal. The blood pressure cuff attached to Joshua's left arm would automatically inflate at regular times and a pulse oximeter would continuously measure the oxygen levels in his blood.

Jeff felt as if his main task was to keep the world at bay for Joshua; to keep all the stressful situations and difficult decisions on the other side of the heavy steel hospital door!

Once again, Jeff was surprised at how protective he felt toward his son-in-law. Perhaps the boy reminded him of how he had been eight months before when the stresses and strains of life had increased to the point where they had been truly unbearable and Jeff had collapsed emotionally.

Now it seemed as if his son-in-law was in danger of not an emotional, but a physical, collapse.

There was a small light on in the room and Jeff could easily make out Joshua's features. His eyes were closed and his breathing was steady and deep.

They were different in a lot of ways. Twenty-plus years between them, and then there was perhaps the most obvious difference, at least to a casual observer: Joshua was Native American and Jeff was Caucasian.

They had a lot in common though. Missy bound them together, Jeff with his father's love, and Joshua with a husband's love.

They were bound together in their grief as well. Jeff's father, Tom Peters, had been like a father to Joshua and his death had thrust Joshua into the heavy and unfamiliar responsibility of owning the lodge and fulfilling alone the shared vision of a youth program.

For Jeff, his father's death had come at a time when he was trying unsuccessfully to come to terms with the fact that his wife was losing the battle with cancer. *He* was losing the battle with cancer. A doctor and he couldn't even save the one he loved most in all the world…

Physician—heal thyself!

It had preyed on his mind day after day as he had watched her slowly fade away. *Physician—heal thyself!*

He hadn't been able to heal that part of himself that had become so deeply entwined with his own heart and soul that he didn't know where one of them stopped and the other began.

Jenny...

Maybe if he'd had someone to lean on during those terrible first days and weeks after she'd died. He'd always been a family man. Any time that he could grasp away from his busy schedule as head of the neo-natal unit, he had spent with his wife and girls—or with his extended family, when he got a chance to actually take a few days vacation and leave the city.

After his wife's death, everyone had suddenly seemed distant, preoccupied or busy with their own grief.

He could see the same pattern of events in his son-in-law's life. One thing after another bearing down on him without any chance to recover in between. And other people around him preoccupied and busy with their own very real difficulties. Jeff regretted that he had been one of those people.

He wanted to change that now. He had truly meant what he'd said to Joshua earlier that day. He wanted to be there for Missy and him. He would help to ease the load on them—instead of adding to it, as he had inadvertently been doing this past winter.

Jeff would want it to be clear that he wasn't trying to "take back" anything that his father had willed to Joshua. Jeff had never for a moment resented that Joshua had inherited the lion's share of his father's wealth. Jeff had money enough. It wasn't money that he needed or wanted.

What he wanted—what he *really* wanted—was for Jenny to be alive and well again. But that wasn't going to happen. And Jeff knew that he needed to pour his heart and mind into something—and someone—else. He had been surprised at the depth of joy that he had felt for his granddaughters. It was different even than what he had felt for his own daughters, burdened as he had been with all the insecurities and doubts of a new father.

Joshua must be experiencing this, too. A new father—of a seven-year-old! That must be quite a challenge! And a baby on the way...

Joshua began to move restlessly about and Jeff laid a comforting hand on his arm. "It's all right, son. Go back to sleep now. Everything's okay..."

"Missy..." Joshua mumbled; his eyes still closed but his face pinched tight with anxiety.

"She's asleep," Jeff said in a soothing voice. "Missy's asleep."

Suddenly Joshua's eyes flew open. "Cynarra!"

"She's okay, too," Jeff assured him. "Cynarra and Keiron are both at the lodge. They're having supper with my mom and Katherine. They're okay. Everyone's doing fine. You can go back to sleep."

Joshua's vision cleared and the tension in his features relaxed.

As Joshua's eyes fluttered shut, Jeff thought about the ones he had left behind at the lodge.

He wondered how Katherine was doing...

He had thought he would never be interested in another woman again. How could any other woman even begin to compare with his beloved Jenny?

But there was no need to compare. They were two different women coming at different times of his life. When he had met Jenny, he had been young and full of enthusiasm for the future. Now, he was older and looking back with some regrets and still lingering vestiges of grief. If Katherine could love and accept him...

Jeff shook his thoughts free. He was jumping way ahead! He hardly knew her. He didn't even know for sure that she wasn't married! She had mentioned a son...

The sound of the outer door opening brought Jeff to his feet in an instant. He darted across the room and grabbed onto the handle, prepared to shut out an unwelcome intruder.

Chapter 8

THE STARTLED LOOK ON JAMIE'S face drew an instant apology from him, but still Jeff stepped toward her and began to pull the door shut behind him.

Jamie, in her nurse's uniform, smiled sardonically at him. "I'd heard you'd appointed yourself Josh's bodyguard." She passed him a tray with various food items on it. "The sandwich and veggies are for you. Josh gets all the good stuff: pudding, Jell-O, fruit cup…"

Jeff nodded. When Joshua next woke up, he'd try to get him to eat a little.

Jamie's face grew serious again. "I really appreciate how you helped Amy today."

Jeff smiled. "She's my granddaughter, too."

Jamie tilted her head thoughtfully. "Yes, I suppose, even more than she is mine."

Jeff shook his head. "It'll soon be official. Those two kids of ours seem pretty intent on getting hitched."

"They wanted to wait until you could be at the wedding," Jamie said softly.

"I'll be there," Jeff promised.

Tears misted Jamie's eyes as she smiled at him. "It's really, really good to have you back, Jeff," she said. "I think a lot of us were afraid that we'd lost you for good."

Jeff nodded, for a moment too overcome to speak. He had so very nearly "been lost for good."

"Better get back to your guard duties," Jamie quipped. "And enjoy your supper."

Jeff gave her a small salute and turned back into the room, a grin on his face. It was good to be back. He'd lived the last eight months in a shadowy world of memories and had all but forgotten what great friends he had back in the real world.

He surveyed the food that Jamie had brought, separating out the "good stuff" for Joshua. The small Health Center didn't often have overnight patients, so food was typically ordered from the local hotel diner. Jeff was happy to see that the sandwich was a corned beef on rye, his favorite. He took it with him to eat in the chair at Joshua's bedside.

The young man, in sleep, looked even younger and more vulnerable.

Jeff remembered the summer he had first met Joshua. If he'd had to use two words to describe the fourteen-year-old, he would have said: "brave" and "loyal." He'd stuck by his friend, Colin, through community opposition and he'd even faced down an angry group of armed men, again in defense of Colin, who was injured and unable to defend himself.

Missy had probably fallen in love with him that summer, though they hadn't gotten married until almost seven years later. They had emailed, talked for hours on the phone and spent every waking moment of their summers together. After Missy had graduated, she'd moved up to Rabbit Lake, and stayed at the lodge with her grandparents. It hadn't been long after that they'd gotten engaged.

Jeff hadn't been supportive of the marriage. Now, looking back, he regretted his harsh criticism of Joshua. In some ways, it had been a type of prejudice, he supposed. Not racial, but social. He'd felt that Joshua wouldn't know how to be a good husband because he'd come from such a rough background of alcohol, drugs and violence. And Jeff had thought that Joshua wouldn't make a good father since he hadn't had a good one himself.

He hadn't taken into account the years that Joshua had spent at the lodge being mentored by Tom—and mothered by Martha. Their love and Joshua's growing awareness of God's love had shaped him into a young man who was more than worthy to be his daughter's husband.

Jeff didn't know why he hadn't seen it at the time. Maybe because he had been in such a state of crisis… his wife was dying, his father had just died… and Joshua had inherited everything.

Jeff had argued with the lawyers about the will. Joshua hadn't even been married to Missy at the time. Tom Peters had willed the entire property and a substantial amount of his money to someone who wasn't even a family member.

Even Joshua's family had turned against him, disappointed that Joshua was not planning to share the wealth with them.

His family was still fighting against him, if his Aunt Yvonne was any indication. Jeff didn't think he'd ever met an angrier, more vicious woman in his life. Why anyone would entrust children to her care, was a mystery to him.

If he had anything to say about it, Cynarra would never be under that roof again, even for a few minutes. How Joshua had survived for all those years, Jeff had no idea.

But it had affected him and subsequent years of loving care from Tom and Martha hadn't completely erased the scars. That was clearly evidenced by how ready Joshua had been to believe that

Missy could leave him. Missy, who had loved him so steadfastly ever since she'd met him when he was only fourteen...

This time the noise at the door was loud and forceful. Jeff was unable to get there in time to prevent Yvonne Quill's entrance. He quickly shut the bedroom door and met her halfway across the room.

Others had arrived in her wake. Jamie and Dr. Smith and, surprisingly, Andrew.

"I have every right to see him," Yvonne shouted. "He's my nephew. You can't stop me." She swore loudly to add emphasis to her words.

Jeff heard the monitors in Joshua's room begin to beep and suddenly was consumed by a rage equal to Yvonne's.

"Get out of here!" he yelled.

Jamie stepped between Yvonne and Jeff; and Dr. Smith and Andrew each took one of Yvonne's arms.

Jamie was only inches away from her. "Not now, Yvonne," she said in a clear, firm voice, meeting the challenge in her eyes with quiet authority.

Yvonne allowed herself to be led back toward the door, but even though she knew she was defeated, or perhaps because she did know, Yvonne continued unabated in an angry tirade against Jeff until they had finally reached the hallway and Jeff closed the door upon them.

He ran back into the bedroom to find Joshua struggling to get out of bed.

Jeff gently put his hands on Joshua's shoulders and eased him back down onto the pillows. "She's gone," he said.

"I—I should talk to her..."

"No," Jeff said firmly as he straightened the covers over Joshua again. "That really wouldn't be a good idea just now."

Jeff could still see, and hear, that the younger man was upset.

"Josh," he said gently, "you have to calm down, son. Take some slow, deep breaths. Look at me. Okay now…"

Jeff held Joshua's eyes with his own as he took a long, deep breath and then another, making sure that Joshua did the same.

After a minute or two, Jeff glanced over at the monitors and was glad to see that Joshua's vital signs were back within normal range again.

"You can't let her get to you like that, man," Jeff said softly.

Joshua groaned and closed his eyes.

It was Jeff's second confrontation with Yvonne in one day. The first time, he'd had Katherine with him. She'd stood up to the older woman in a cool, confident way, demanding that the children be released to come with them. Yvonne had yelled profanities at them—in two languages. The children had cowered far out of reach and Jeff's anger had grown with each passing moment. Katherine, through it all, kept calm and cool. *They were here for the children. They were going to leave now with the children.*

They had driven down in a truck. There was plenty of room for the four of them in the cab; the children were both quite small and Katherine was slim also.

It had been a quiet ride back to the lodge. Cynarra held tightly onto Katherine's hand. Jeff thought that everyone would relax again once the children were back with Joshua and Missy.

He hadn't expected to find Joshua critically ill. The children had looked, if possible, even more frightened than before.

When Jeff had called earlier, they seemed to be doing okay. Martha, at least, was familiar to both of them. And Katherine…

Jeff glanced over at Joshua. The young man's eyes were still closed. The monitor alarms were silent and the flashing numbers were reassuring. Jeff moved out into the other room, picked up the phone, and dialed.

His mother answered, anxious to know how Joshua was doing. Jeff gave her a full progress report and then asked about Missy and the children. He was told that Missy was still asleep, justifiably exhausted by her ordeal, and that Charles was entertaining the children with a new computer game.

"So you're planning to spend the night there, too?" his mom asked.

"Yeah, there's a couch here that pulls out into a bed. I'll use that."

"Is there anything else you need… your suitcase… or do you have that with you?"

"No, think I just dropped it inside the lodge door when I first arrived—it's probably still there," Jeff replied.

There was a bit of a mumbled sound and then Martha said, "Katherine's offered to drop your bag off to you on her way back to the hotel."

Jeff tried to control the rising bubble of joy that he knew would be so easily detected by his mother. "Yes," he said formally, "that would be fine. And please tell Ms. Blake-Jones that I appreciate her taking the trouble…"

He was interrupted by a peal of laughter. "Tell her yourself!" Martha said, as she hung up the phone.

Jeff shook his head and grinned, too happy at the prospect of seeing Katherine again to be dismayed by his mother's reaction. A notorious matchmaker, Martha was probably even now, boring Katherine with stories of Jeff's exploits. As long as she didn't pull out the baby pictures!

He was still smiling as he walked back into Joshua's room.

Jeff's smile broadened as he noted that Joshua had his eyes open and was once again looking relaxed. There was even a spark of humor in the young man's eyes as he asked, "Win the lottery?"

"Nope!" Jeff purposely checked his hair in the mirror before dropping into a chair beside the bed.

Joshua grinned at him. "Meeting someone special?"

"Yep!"

"Gonna tell me about it?"

Jeff considered a moment then grinned. "Nope." It was one thing to think about the possibility of getting to know Katherine better; quite another thing to talk about it. But it seemed as if his mother had already sensed that he and Katherine were attracted to each other...

"So, you're just going to abandon me?" Joshua spoke with feigned chagrin.

"Nope!" Jeff continued the light bantering. "Can't get rid of me that easily. Besides, she's coming over here—" Jeff broke off as Joshua grinned broadly.

"Just to bring over my suitcase. It's not like it's a date or anything..." Jeff felt his face grow red.

Joshua laughed. Then his brow furrowed a little. "Katherine? Are you talking about Katherine? Isn't she a little young for you?"

It was Jeff's turn to laugh. "And just how old do you think I am?"

Joshua bit his lip and looked sheepish. "Sorry."

"I'm forty-nine," Jeff said pointedly, "not eighty-nine."

"Sorry," Joshua said again but Jeff was pleased to see that he was grinning as he said it. As a doctor, Jeff knew the value of humor, and agreed with the Bible's assertion that laughter was as good as medicine.

Jeff leaned back and put his hands behind his head. "And if I've got it figured right," he continued, "Katherine should be around thirty-nine or maybe even forty."

"Still think you're robbing the cradle," Joshua quipped.

Jeff was pleased that Joshua felt comfortable enough to joke with him—and well enough to do so. He stood to his feet. "Feel like eating something?"

Joshua grimaced. "Not really."

"C'mon," Jeff said encouragingly, "I'll help you to sit up. You can make your decision after that."

Jeff put his arms under Joshua's shoulders and hoisted him up into a sitting position then arranged the pillows comfortably behind his back.

In the end he was able to persuade Joshua to drink some juice and eat a fruit cup, a Jell-O, and a pudding. "That should give you a great sugar high, if nothing else," Jeff declared.

"Must have been hungry after all," Joshua said, surveying the empty containers on his tray.

"Must've been," Jeff agreed with a grin. "Do you want to keep sitting up for a while or would you like to lie down again?"

Joshua considered the question and answered, "I could sit for a little bit, maybe."

Jeff checked his vital signs and took a look in Joshua's throat. It was difficult to know if it was marginally better or not. It would take time for the antibiotic to work.

Jeff wondered if talking about it would be a help to the young man. He began in a casual voice, "So... you've been under a bit of stress lately."

Joshua lowered his eyes and nodded.

Jeff was puzzled by this response and wondered if Joshua viewed the current difficulties in his life as evidence of personal failure.

He decided to try a different angle. "Sometimes, it seems that when it rains, it pours," he said.

Joshua looked up. "Yeah."

"Wanna talk about it?" Jeff offered.

But Joshua shook his head. "I don't think that would help much. It's not just one thing. It's—*everything!*"

Jeff grinned and raised an eyebrow. "That's a lot."

"Yeah." Joshua was able to smile back at him. "I guess it's like what you said about the rain, only the roof is leaking too. I get a bucket under one leak and I hear some dripping coming from another spot of the house and while I'm running to get a pail under that one—"

Jeff laughed and said, "I get the idea," but his smile faded as he saw the sadness return to Joshua's eyes.

"It just seems as if I can't do anything right. But I can't quit either. You can't just quit being a husband or a father. And I can't just quit my job at the lodge because I own it! Sometimes…" Joshua's voice fell to a whisper. "Sometimes, I think everyone would be better off without me."

Jeff shook his head. "No, they wouldn't," he said.

Joshua fingered the edge of the blanket, avoiding Jeff's eyes as he spoke. "Tom shouldn't have given me all that money. Someone else could have done a better job with it. And—and I shouldn't have married Missy. She should have married someone else—someone who could better care for her and our children."

"Hmm…" Jeff said. "Sounds like something I might have said eight or nine months ago."

"And you were right!" Joshua said, his voice trembling and his eyes on fire.

"No," Jeff said in a quiet confident voice. "I was wrong, Josh."

"But I've failed!" Joshua spoke fiercely. "I've failed at everything!"

Jeff shook his head. This past winter, he had been caught like a fly in a spider's web of grief. He had been unable to move; unable to help himself; but he had still been able, to some degree, to observe the world around him. "I've been watching you," he said gently. "You have more than proved yourself capable as a strong and loving husband to my daughter. And I *know* that my father would have been so proud of what you'd accomplished with the youth program in such a short amount of time. He'd been dreaming about getting that project off the ground for years. And you've been a father to Cynarra for how many days?"

"About a week," Joshua said faintly.

"And if there was ever a little girl that loved her daddy…"

"How's she doing?" Joshua asked. "She looked so worried. I wish I could see her. And—and Missy…"

"Missy is still asleep," Jeff said gently. "Hopefully, she'll sleep right through the night. But Cynarra should still be up. It's not that late. Maybe she could come over for a short visit."

Joshua eyes flared with hope. "I thought I couldn't have any visitors."

Jeff chuckled. "Well, none like your Aunt Yvonne, that's for sure."

Joshua lowered his eyes.

Jeff gave him a gentle nudge in his arm. "Hey," he said, "let me call the lodge and see if Cynarra can come over."

There was a phone at the bedside table, but Jeff went to the other room to make the call. There seemed to be no end of fresh trouble at the lodge and if there was another "hole in the roof" that had started to leak through, Jeff didn't want anything that he said or did to indicate the situation to Joshua.

He was determined to do what Dr. Phillips had advised two days ago when Joshua was released from the hospital. No extra stress!

Jeff was delighted when Katherine agreed to bring Cynarra over for a quick visit when she dropped off Jeff's suitcase.

He walked grinning back into Joshua's room. "They're coming right over."

Joshua's eyebrow shot up. "They?"

Jeff just couldn't stop smiling. "Yeah, Katherine and Cynarra."

Joshua waved his arm toward the other room. "Well, you two can visit out there," he teased. "I don't know if my heart can handle the excitement of having you both in the same room at the same time."

Jeff smiled good-naturedly. "Actually, she probably won't come in here at all. We're bending the rules a bit for Cynarra and even her visit will need to be kept short. Ten minutes tops."

JEFF'S HEART GAVE A FEW bounding leaps when Katherine appeared. It was hard to believe that he had just met her.

Jeff tried to restrain his runaway emotions. He didn't really know anything about her. No, that wasn't true. He'd learned a lot in the brief time that they'd been thrown together. He'd learned that she had courage and intelligence—and she was very beautiful.

Cynarra was no longer frightened or timid. She walked past Jeff towards the open door. "Is my daddy in here?"

Jeff nodded. "Yes, and he's very anxious to see you."

Cynarra didn't wait for him but walked boldly into the family room and on into the adjoining patient's room.

Jeff saw Joshua's face light up with joy and relief, and knew he had done the right thing allowing Cynarra to visit.

Jeff walked back to where Katherine was waiting in the hallway. "Think I'll just give them a bit of time," he said.

"I'll wait and bring her back, if you want," Katherine offered. "Martha said that she was sure Joshua and Missy wouldn't mind if I borrowed the camp van."

Jeff smiled. "Yes, that'd be great if you could wait and bring Cynarra home. Uh… Maybe I'll grab a couple of chairs…"

He set the two chairs side-by-side against the corridor wall. From where he sat, he could still see into the main room and even glimpse a corner of the room where Joshua's bed was and for sure, he would be able to hear if the cardiac monitor alarm went off.

They both sat down and suddenly, Jeff felt an unreasonable surge of panic.

What in the world was he going to say to her? Why had he set the chairs side-by-side like patients in a waiting room? What was he going to say to her?

"Are you married?"

Oh, man! Had he really said that? Jeff ducked his head in embarrassment.

"Not at the moment," came the slightly amused but still gracious reply.

Jeff dared to look up at her. "I'm sorry," he said. "You must think…"

"I think it's a very reasonable question under the circumstances," Katherine said with a smile.

"Cir-circumstances…?" *Jeff couldn't believe it. He was acting like a tongue-tied schoolboy!*

Katherine laughed and moved her chair so that they were at a more comfortable angle for conversation. Their knees met and Jeff felt even that slight touch go through his body like a jolt of electricity.

"I do want to tell you about myself…" Katherine began.

Her mellow, almost husky voice, set his heart racing and it took a moment for Jeff to realize that the conversation had taken on a more serious note.

"My husband died five years ago."

"I'm so sorry," Jeff said with deep compassion, knowing firsthand the pain of losing a life partner.

Katherine smiled fragilely. "It was a difficult time. Our little boy was only two—he doesn't remember his daddy at all."

Jeff realized, with a feeling of gratitude, that his daughters both had good memories of a long and happy relationship with their mother.

"We had waited a long time to have children," Katherine continued in a slow, sad voice. "We thought our lives were too dangerous…"

Katherine paused and looked up at him to explain, "I was a war correspondent and my husband the cameraman. We were a team."

"It's funny," Katherine said with a trace of bitterness in her voice, "we waited to have kids till we were back 'safe' in America and less than four years later, my husband was killed in a drugstore robbery in the middle of one of the safest sections of the city. He had just gone to pick up some cough medicine for our son…"

Katherine broke off, too overcome to speak.

Jeff could see that her knuckles were white from gripping the side of the chair. He reached out and took her hand. "I know how you feel," he said.

"Yes." Katherine nodded thoughtfully. "Yes, you do. And I shouldn't be dumping my troubles on you. It hasn't been that long for you, has it?"

Jeff shook his head. "Nine months. But I can't imagine a time when I won't miss Jenny; nine months or nine years… She'll always be a part of me."

"What's going on here?"

Jeff looked up to see his daughter's angry flushed cheeks and flaming eyes as she strode toward them.

He quickly released Katherine's hand and stood to his feet.

"Missy…" he said.

Chapter 9

Joshua heard Missy's voice ring high and clear. "What do you mean I can't see my husband? Cynarra can see him. You can see him. Even this woman—"

"Honey, you just need to calm down first," Jeff said in quieter tones.

Joshua hoped that his father-in-law would be able to defuse some of Missy's anger before he had to face her.

He'd been talking to Cynarra about her time at Yvonne's, wishing with all of his heart that he could have done something to prevent the little girl from experiencing such trauma. Cynarra seemed so resilient but Joshua wanted to keep the dialogue open with her, letting her know that she could speak with him about her experience at any time.

Missy appeared in the doorway and suddenly all Joshua's thoughts were consumed by her.

She'd thrown a coat on over her pajamas; her hair was in disarray; and her eyes were brimming with tears.

"Missy…" he tried to whisper past the lump in his throat.

"No one told me…" Her voice caught on a sob. "No one woke me to tell me…"

"It's okay. I'm okay."

She sank onto the bed beside him and fell weeping into his arms.

Joshua barely noticed Jeff speaking gently to Cynarra then ushering her out of the room.

He held Missy tightly, speaking words of comfort.

"I'm sorry, Josh," he heard her say.

But it was he who had wronged *her*. "Missy, *I'm* sorry," he said.

She sat up and Joshua's arms fell away.

"I should have looked for you instead—instead of thinking you were gone."

Missy shook her head. "Why would you—how could you—even begin to imagine…?"

"Missy, I'm so sorry."

"But why, Josh?"

He turned away from all the love and sorrow he saw in her eyes. "I don't know," he began. "I think, maybe, I've been feeling lately as if I've failed at everything. I was sure that our marriage was failing, too."

Missy reached for a Kleenex from the bedside table, wiped at her eyes and blew her nose. "It's my fault," she said. "I've been so grumpy."

Joshua stroked her face, pushing back some wet strands of hair. "It wasn't your fault, Missy. I should never have doubted your love."

Missy lowered her eyes. "I just feel like throwing up all the time."

"Oh, sweetheart, I'm so sorry."

Missy smiled wanly. "Well, that's not all your fault. I guess it was a bit of a joint effort."

Joshua had to smile at that. Yeah, he guessed it had been. But he wished that the pregnancy wasn't so hard on Missy. "How are you feeling now?" he asked.

"I'm doing good," Missy said. "After I drank a couple of gallons of water, I had a long soaking bath, Grandma stuffed me full of great food, and then I had the longest nap in recorded history. I must have slept for at least four or five hours."

Her face clouded over as she continued, "I was a bit upset that they didn't bother to wake me when my husband was rushed into the hospital."

Joshua squeezed her hand. "You needed your sleep, honey." He hesitated before asking, "So… our baby is okay?"

Missy smiled broadly. "Yes, he's fine. Grandma found my dad's old stethoscope lying around and…" Missy paused for effect and then spoke as if making a special proclamation, "…I heard his heartbeat!"

Joshua laughed. "Whose heartbeat?"

"Our baby's!" Missy exclaimed joyously. "Who do you think?"

"You said *he*," Joshua teased.

Missy nodded. "Grandma said that if the baby's heartbeat is under 140, that means that it's a boy."

Joshua grinned. A boy sounded just fine to him.

"A little brother for Cynarra," Missy said softly.

Cynarra… How was she?

Missy must have read Joshua's thoughts. "I'll check on her," she said.

Missy came back into the room a few minutes later. "Katherine drove her back to the lodge. Dad said we weren't to worry. And he talked to Grandma, and she said she'd stay with Cynarra and Keiron as long as I needed her to. And Dad said that he thought it would be okay if I stayed and visited with you a while longer."

Joshua smiled. "That'd be great."

JEFF WAS THRILLED THAT KATHERINE had come back to the Health Center to see him after dropping off Cynarra.

He was in the nursery checking on Amy's progress when she got there.

The little girl's color was good, her vitals stable and her oxygen levels higher than before.

"May I have a photo of the two of you?" Katherine asked.

Jeff gently lifted the baby up against the clean white gown he had put on.

Katherine took several pictures and even as Jeff laid Amy back down and rechecked all the equipment and the baby's vitals, Katherine kept on snapping photos.

Jeff spoke to the attending nurse, said goodnight to his granddaughter and finally turned toward Katherine. "You're taking a lot of pictures," he commented.

Her eyes were shining. "Some of this equipment was from the original 'Rachel's Children' operation, wasn't it?"

"Yes," Jeff said slowly, "some of it."

Katherine was looking eagerly around, her camera poised and ready in her hands. "Can you show me?"

Jeff couldn't keep the sadness from his voice. "Not right now," he said.

"But..." Something in his manner must have finally got through to her for Katherine fell silent as Jeff took off his white gown and ushered her out of the nursery.

"Lets talk out here," he said.

Jeff looped his arm through hers and led her into the doctor's office.

He automatically took the chair behind the desk and waved Katherine toward the visitor's chair. Jeff's heart felt so heavy, he could barely speak the words, "Why are you here?"

Katherine smiled faintly and took the time to put her camera and notebook back into her large black leather shoulder bag.

Anger suddenly replaced sadness, as Jeff demanded, "Who are you? Who do you work for? What's your angle?"

Katherine set the bag carefully down beside her chair. When she lifted her eyes up again, they no longer shone with excitement and enthusiasm.

"So many questions…" she said in a slow, sad voice.

"You're a reporter."

Katherine laughed shakily. "The way you said that like 'you're an assassin' or 'you're a terrorist'."

Jeff sighed. "Same thing, I guess. You're a destroyer of people's lives."

"What!" Katherine exclaimed, angrily jumping to her feet.

Jeff knew he had gone too far but half-buried resentments from the past reared their ugly heads as he continued on. "You don't care about who you hurt. If it makes a good story, that's all that matters."

Katherine bent down to pick up her bag. When she raised her head, her face was flushed and her eyes filled with tears. She put the van keys on the desk and said, "I'll walk to the hotel. It's not that far."

But Jeff still felt as if he needed to make it quite clear. "If you write anything about my personal life or any of my family members…"

He was talking to an empty room. Katherine was gone.

She'd just been after a story—all the time she was pretending to be a friend—and perhaps more than a friend.

He'd certainly given her the "human element"—the "personal touch"—or whatever they called it. Telling her all about his family...

Katherine told you about herself too, Jeff's heart argued.

That's what reporters do—tell you some of their story to show they empathize—and then you'll tell them even more!

And his grandchildren... She was so anxious to take pictures of them. And she'd spent the morning over at Sandy Point—and perhaps the evening before. She'd probably heard the whole story of how the children were born as the result of a rape. If she got the story published then those kids would have to live with that for the rest of their lives—that everyone else knew about it! And Andrew and Jasmine's relationship—what would happen to that?

No, Andrew wasn't the type to let things like that bother him. He'd stand by Jasmine, no matter what.

But it wasn't fair to the children.

And he certainly didn't want Missy to have her picture splashed all over the pages. She'd had enough of that already—thanks to Katherine's father!

He'd had enough of it too. All those years of being in the shadow of his NBA star father. All his life, Jeff had endured the speculations, questions and comments from reporters who couldn't ever stop wondering why Tom Peters had adopted a little white boy.

Reporters...

Jenny had written articles and published a book, too. She had worked with Dylan McPherson to expose Rachel's Children. She had been ready to sacrifice her relationship with Jeff—and even his possible conviction and prison sentence—all for the sake of her story. It had turned out all right but it could just as easily have not.

She hadn't written much after they were married. His job had demanded increasingly more time and the children had needed her attention.

Jeff's thoughts grew darker and more confused as the moments passed. He felt himself slipping down into the quagmire of past memories and regrets.

For the first time in weeks, he thought about using mood-altering drugs. He was back in the Health Center. Only a few steps away... Jeff felt a deep physical craving for the release and rest that the pills could offer.

"It's that reporter lady."

"Where do you want her?"

Jeff heard the man's voice and the woman's reply, their words carrying down the short hallway and through the open door of the examination room.

In an instant, Jeff was on his feet and running.

Katherine! Something had happened to Katherine!

She was being held between two police officers like a criminal —or a drunk. Her head lolled forward. Her clothes were torn and dirty, her hair a tangled mess.

"Why isn't she on a stretcher?" Jeff demanded.

"She said she could walk," one of the female police officers protested.

Jeff stepped forward. "Let me..." he said, putting his arm around Katherine's waist. The young constable moved away. Katherine leaned into Jeff's shoulder and he could feel her trembling —from cold or fright or maybe a physical reaction to the trauma.

The other police officer stepped away, too, and Jeff felt Katherine begin to sag. He quickly bent and slipped a hand under her knees and lifted her up into his arms. "You should have called for medical support," Jeff spoke over his shoulder as he carried her toward a treatment room.

"In cases where the victim is still ambulatory..." the young officer began.

Jeff didn't hear the rest. All his focus was on Katherine. "I'm sorry," he whispered in her ear. He wasn't sure if she was in any condition to receive his apology, but he'd say it now and he'd say it again later and tomorrow and the day after.

He laid her gently down on the stretcher, but as he released her, Katherine reached up quickly and grabbed hold of his arm. Jeff pulled a stool over and sat down, trying in vain to distance himself enough to think like a doctor. The first thing was a quick preliminary assessment. Her breathing was okay.

She was crying!

There was some blood from an abrasion on her cheek and bruises but there didn't seem to be any other external bleeding... *No... there seeping through her sweater!* Jeff felt her pain as if it was his own.

Jamie was cutting away the piece of sweater. The incision was just above Katherine's waist... *Thank God, it didn't look too deep.* Katherine must have dodged her assailant. It would need a couple of stitches, though. *Clean it first...*

"Saline solution..." Jeff ordered in a voice that trembled.

Jamie lifted her head. There was a strange look in her eyes as she said the words, "I know." She turned toward the nurse beside her. "Call Dr. Smith. Knife wound. Not life threatening."

Jeff half-rose to his feet. "I can..." But his voice once more betrayed him. He sounded as weak and shaky as he felt. He sank back down onto the stool and focused all his attention on Katherine. She was turned on her side toward him and her hair had fallen over her face. Gently, Jeff lifted away the strands that were adhering to the tears on her face.

"It's going to be okay," he said tenderly.

She tried to smile a little, but her lips were trembling.

"It's okay," he said, feeling his stomach churn and his heart wrench at the sight of her. "Who did this to you?" he asked in a hoarse voice.

"We'd like to know that, too," a voice said from behind them. Jeff turned and saw the older of the two police officers.

The constable addressed Katherine, "Did you see any of their faces, ma'am?"

She winced and turned her head in toward Jeff's arm. He could feel her warm tears and instinctively, Jeff placed his other arm around her. "She can talk to you later," he said.

Jamie came around to stand beside Jeff. "You can interview the patient after she's received treatment for her injuries," Jamie said authoritatively.

Jeff didn't bother to look to see if the police officer had left or not; he kept his eyes focused on Katherine, wishing there was something he could do to help.

"Jeff," Jamie said, "I need you to go and check on Joshua first and then go check on Amy. She may be due for a feeding; there's a chart beside her incubator."

Jeff started to protest, but Jamie was speaking to Katherine now, gently extricating her hands from Jeff's and holding them in her own. "Okay, honey, I need you to focus on me, now. Jeff needs to go for just a minute..."

No, I don't!

"Jeff..." Jamie spoke in gentle reproof.

He tore his eyes away from Katherine's face and stood to his feet. The other nurse was just removing the patient's shoes and socks. Katherine's right ankle looked swollen and bruised.

"They made her walk on that!" Jeff exploded.

"The cruiser was pulled right up to the door," Jamie said calmly. "And I'm sure if they'd known…"

"Jeff…"

His heart lurched at the sound of his name from Katherine's lips.

The tenderness in her voice was unmistakable but so was her message. "Please go," she said.

Jeff turned and stumbled out of the room, confused at first about where he should go and what he should do. Then he remembered. Amy… And Joshua…

He headed toward the family room first. It was dark and quiet, and at first Jeff thought that Missy must have gone home. Then he saw her quietly sitting beside Joshua's bed, holding his hand.

She must have heard him come in. She turned to glance at her father then slowly extricated her hand from Joshua's and quietly walked out of the small room into the larger one.

"I guess I should go home," she said in a sleepy voice. Then she looked closely at him and asked, "What's wrong?"

Jeff motioned for her to come out into the hallway where they would be sure not to disturb Joshua.

"It's Katherine," he said. "She was attacked… on her way to her hotel." He couldn't keep his voice from trembling.

Missy stared at him. "Katherine? The reporter?"

Jeff felt deep anguish and remorse. "None of that matters now. I—I have to go check on her. Jamie said to check on Joshua but he's okay. And I just saw Amy…"

Missy was still staring at him as if he had two heads. Suddenly, her face melted into a smile of compassion. "I'll go check on her, Dad. You stay with Josh, okay?"

She took his arm and led him back into the family room to an easy chair. "I just made a pot of tea," she said. "I was going to give some to Josh but he was already asleep by the time it was ready."

Missy pressed a cup of tea into his hands and kissed him gently on the forehead. "Don't worry," she said.

He tried to relax but found it impossible to do so. He felt as if he'd been waiting a long time before Missy returned, stepping quietly over to shut the door to Joshua's room before sitting down on the sofa adjacent to him.

"She's fine," Missy said. "Jamie said that we should give them a few more minutes. She's going to need some stitches on that knife wound."

Jeff lurched to his feet, spilling tea on his jeans. His heart was beating fast. "Stitches?" he said in a trembling voice. Then he willed himself to be calm; he'd known she would need stitches.

"How—how many?" he asked.

Missy smiled gently at him. "I don't know, Daddy. But she's going to be okay—really."

Jeff eased down onto the chair again. "How long did Jamie say?"

"A few minutes," Missy said. "Maybe ten."

Jeff glanced at his watch and took a deep breath.

"I apologized to her."

Jeff stared at his daughter. "It wasn't your fault!"

Missy shook her head. "I apologized for being so catty towards her. I—I guess I was just jealous."

"Jealous?" Jeff asked incredulously. "Jealous of Katherine?"

Missy smiled wanly. "I've just been feeling so—so *pregnant* lately."

Jeff grinned at her. He just couldn't help it. "Well..."

Missy sighed, and Jeff stopped smiling as she continued, "I've been so tired. And I feel like throwing up all the time..."

Jeff took her hand in his. "Oh, honey."

"She just looked so perfect. Every hair in place... her makeup flawless... her clothes—"

"You're usually like that too," Jeff protested.

Missy grinned wryly and glanced down at her robe and pajamas. "*Usually* is the key word here," she quipped.

"Now honey, that's not what I meant."

"No, it's okay," she said with a reassuring smile. "I haven't been myself lately but that was no reason to be jealous of Katherine or to resent the time she spent with Joshua."

"She spent time with Joshua?"

Missy waved her hand dismissively. "Yeah, she had so many questions about Rachel's Children and about the camp. She wanted to do an article about where everyone was now—or something like that."

"I know," Jeff said quietly. "I told her that she couldn't do it. I didn't want her writing about any of my family. I thought we'd had enough of all that."

Missy looked puzzled. "But that was years ago, Dad. I don't think it would hurt to talk about it now. All the legalities were ironed out a long time ago, weren't they?"

"Yes. Yes, they were." He shook his head. "I guess I thought there was something developing between us—and then I found out she was only after a story. And now, I don't know..."

Missy smiled warmly at him. "I don't think she's just after a story, Dad."

Jeff glanced at his watch and stood resolutely to his feet. "I need to apologize to her. It's all my fault that she was out walking this late at night—and got attacked."

Missy said, "There's still some tea left. Did you want to bring a cup down for Katherine?"

KATHERINE WAS HOPING THAT JEFF would stop by soon. The pain medication they'd given her was starting to take effect and she was beginning to feel very drowsy.

She heard a sound at the door and looked up hopefully. But it was just two police officers coming to question her. One of them, the woman, was of the original pair that had brought her to the Health Center. The other one, an older man, was someone she hadn't seen before.

His voice was kind as he asked, "Did you get a look at their faces?"

Katherine shuddered. Maybe it was the kindness in his voice that broke through her defenses. Tears started to trickle down her cheeks. "Yes," she said in a trembling voice.

They would haunt her dreams for years to come. Whenever she tried to close her eyes…

"Can you describe them?"

"Yes," she said, bowing her head, ashamed of the tremor she could not keep from her voice.

"We will speak with you again in the morning."

Katherine looked up in surprise.

"The correct procedure is to interview the alleged victim immediately following the events," said the younger officer in an aggrieved voice. "It is possible she might forget..."

"She won't forget."

Katherine felt a burst of gratitude toward the senior officer and when he stretched out his hand toward her, she gladly accepted his handshake.

"I'm sorry that this had to happen to you in our community," he said, releasing her hand. "Our youth..." His voice trailed off. "The hurts go back generations. Sometimes the solutions are not so easy."

It was an apology!

Katherine nodded solemnly. *Apology accepted.*

Jamie burst into the room at that moment. "Colin! Can't this wait till the morning?"

"Your timing's off," the younger police officer said snidely as she brushed past Jamie on her way out the door.

"Colin..." Jamie said uncertainly.

He turned back to Katherine. "Ten o'clock be okay for you?"

Katherine nodded.

Colin sank down into one of the chairs. "Some of these kids can be helped," he said. "If we can catch them soon enough, clear their brains of drugs and get them into a youth program... We had one running here last winter up at Goldrock Lodge. Joshua Quill did a good job..."

"I've met Joshua," Katherine said softly.

Colin's eyes lit up with interest. "That's right. You're doing a story about Rachel's Children. Are you going to write about the youth program that they're doing now?"

Katherine lowered her eyes. "I was going to."

"Joshua could use some media support right now," Colin said eagerly.

"I'm not really…" Katherine began. "Right now, I'm just a free-lance reporter. Even if I write up the story, I have to convince a newspaper to buy it from me. And…" she added, "my camera was taken last night."

Colin flipped open his notebook, once more a police officer. "What else was taken?" he asked.

Katherine itemized the contents of her bag as Colin wrote them down.

"They'll likely only be interested in the cash. Unless they can find a buyer for the camera…" he added thoughtfully. "I'll get the word out that it's a hot item. We can put it on the radio and people will be on the lookout for it."

"Colin…" Jamie spoke with mild reproof in her voice.

He stood to his feet, grinning. "My big sister," he said in a stage whisper to Katherine. "I'm Chief of Police and she still thinks she can boss me around."

Katherine's smile grew wider as Jeff walked in with two cups of hot drinks in his hands. He glared at Colin. "You can't wait to interview her until tomorrow?" he demanded.

Colin shook his head and chuckled. "Guess I'm leaving you in good hands, Ms. Blake-Jones. See you tomorrow."

He patted a bewildered Jeff on the shoulder and left.

Jamie said, "I'll leave you two alone to talk." Then she was gone, too.

A tidal wave of emotions swept over Jeff as he looked at Katherine. He'd only ever felt this way for one other woman— this crazy, head-over-heels surge of love that all but took his breath away.

"Jeff..." she said tenderly.

But he had to tell her first. He had to tell her...

"I'm sorry," they both said in the same instant.

Jeff set the cups of tea down on the bedside table and sank down into the chair beside her bed.

Katherine tried to raise herself a little and winced in pain. Jeff jumped to his feet. "Don't try to move," he advised. "I'll put the bed up higher for you."

He pressed the button to raise the head of the bed, watching carefully to see at what level she wanted it stopped.

"That's good," she said, when the bed had reached a 45-degree angle. He heard the catch in her breath as she spoke.

"Sure it's not too high?" he asked anxiously.

Katherine smiled faintly. "No, it's okay."

She still didn't look very comfortable. "Here," he said, "Put your arms around my neck." He hooked his arms under her shoulders and hoisted her up higher on the bed. "How's that?" he asked.

"Good," she said softly, taking an extra moment to remove her hands from around his neck.

It had felt so natural, so right, to have her in his arms... *He had almost kissed her!*

"My foot..." she said. "It slipped off the pillow."

Jeff glanced down and realized that she was referring to her sprained ankle. He pulled back the sheet a little and gently lifted her foot onto the high pillow. He glanced quickly up at Katherine, making sure that he hadn't hurt her.

She was holding her breath. She was in pain!

Jeff frantically grabbed at the clipboard hanging from the end of her bed. "What did they give you for pain medication?" he gasped. "They should have given you something strong enough..."

"Jeff…"

"We could up the dose a little. We—"

"Jeff…"

Something in her voice stopped his frantic fumblings and made him focus in on her soft smile and gentle look.

"You brought me some tea…"

Jeff ran a hand through his hair and tried to quiet his racing heart and steady his breathing.

Tea…

He used two hands on the mug, afraid that he might spill it otherwise.

"This is great tea," she said.

"It's not too cold?" he asked anxiously.

"No," she said, taking another sip. "It's okay."

"I forgot to ask—do you take cream or sugar?"

She waited a moment before answering, causing him to stop and focus on her face once more. She smiled serenely and spoke in a slow, calming voice. "It's perfect."

Jeff took a deep breath and sat down again.

"Did you bring a cup for yourself?" Katherine asked, glancing toward the bedside table.

Jeff reached for the tea and took a swallow.

He looked up at Katherine. She was still smiling. But he needed to apologize to her…

"What I said last night…" he began.

"It's okay," she said softly.

"About reporters…"

"It's okay, Jeff," she said with great tenderness in her voice. "We'll work it out."

We'll work it out…

"I don't care what you do for a job…"

Katherine set her tea down on the bedside table and raised her arms. "Actually, could you maybe just lift me a little higher?" she asked. "I seemed to have slipped down just a bit."

Jeff stood quickly to his feet, set the tea sloshing down on the table and bent over the bed. He put his arms under her and lifted. In the same instant, Katherine pulled him closer and Jeff kissed her… as she had intended him to.

Chapter 10

JEFF THOUGHT HE WAS STILL dreaming. Someone was calling, "Dad! Dad!" But it was a man's voice and Jeff only had daughters…

Suddenly, he was wide-awake. *Joshua!*

"Yeah…" he answered, throwing the covers off and reaching for his glasses. "I'm coming," he said, as he stumbled sleepily into Joshua's room.

"I tried calling 'Dr. Peters.' I tried calling 'Jeff.' Finally, I thought I might get your attention if I yelled, 'Dad!' Guess it worked," Joshua said.

Jeff grinned. "I meant what I said. I do want you to call me 'Dad.'"

"Thought you were supposed to sit by my bed all night," Joshua said with a carefree laugh. "Wipe my fevered brow and all that…"

Jeff was happy to see Joshua in such a good mood. "You don't have a fevered brow," he said pointedly. Then he looked closer at the machine monitoring Joshua's vital signs. His temperature was down. The analgesic from the night before would have worn off by now; he was due for another dose soon. Maybe his fever really was gone.

"Let me see your throat," he said, grabbing a flashlight.

He peered into Joshua's throat and gave a satisfied sigh. The antibiotic was taking hold. "That's a lot better," he said.

"Can I get out of bed now?" Joshua asked. "I feel like a prisoner with all this stuff attached to me."

"Now, let's not rush things," Jeff said. "We'll get you sitting up again and you can have breakfast and then we'll see, okay."

Joshua grinned. "Okay."

Jeff checked the IV.

Joshua asked, "Can I call Missy?"

Jeff felt like a taskmaster... or a father. *No, you can't get out of bed yet. Yes, you can call a friend.*

He glanced at his watch: 6:45. "Will she be awake yet?" he asked.

Joshua considered. "Maybe I should wait for her to call."

Jeff grinned. "Maybe." He ran his hand across the stubble on his face. "I think I'll have a shower and shave while the day is yet young."

"Seeing Katherine again?" Joshua teased.

"Well... I'll probably make a full pot of coffee..."

There was a separate bathroom in the family room suite. Jeff didn't take long to shower and get dressed in clean clothes from his overnight bag.

As Jeff repacked his bag, he thought about Katherine. He was grateful that she'd brought his stuff over for him. Maybe he should do the same for her or at least arrange to have it done. Maybe Missy could stop by at the hotel and get Katherine's bags for her.

As Jeff straightened up the room a little and put on a pot of coffee, he continued to think about Katherine. He wondered how she was feeling this morning. Suddenly, he urgently had to know...

He popped his head into Joshua's room. "I'll be right back," he said.

Joshua grinned. "No need to rush. Say hi to her for me."

Jeff heard the gurgling of the coffee machine in the background. He offered Joshua a cup, but Josh said that he was okay. "H_2O is fine for me," he quipped, nodding toward the water carafe on his bedside table.

Jeff poured two cups of coffee and hurried out of the room.

As Missy opened the door to the kitchen, the smells of breakfast filled the air and a strange tableau greeted her. Martha was flipping some pancakes, Charles was leaning against the counter beside her, munching on an apple and Keiron was sitting at the table, pouring syrup on a stack of pancakes.

Missy shook her head and grinned philosophically. It was good to be alive. It was good to have family and friends who cared. What did it matter if the property lines got occasionally blurred?

Charles glanced over at her, grinned and nudged Martha. "Sleeping beauty awakes."

Martha spun around. "Missy, honey, I hope you don't mind. Keiron was awake and…"

Missy walked quickly across the room and embraced her grandmother.

"I've been such a grump," she apologized.

Martha smiled. "How're you feeling?" she asked. "Do you think you could manage some breakfast?"

Missy surprised herself by saying, "Yes." It was hard to believe, but the thought of food didn't make her feel queasy as it usually did. Maybe it had helped that she'd slept through an entire night for a change.

Martha flipped some pancakes onto a plate and handed them to her. Missy sat down beside Keiron, exchanged "good morning's" with him and reached for the syrup. Her stomach rumbled and Missy realized that she was actually hungry. It was a good feeling.

"By the way, Joshua called—twice," her grandmother said. "He told me not to wake you."

Missy immediately forgot about the pancakes as she jumped to her feet, snatched up the phone, and dialed the number for the Health Center.

In the background, she heard Charles chuckling. "Should've told her *after* she ate breakfast."

Missy was transferred through to Joshua's room and he picked up the phone on the first ring.

It was so good to hear his voice. And he sounded so cheerful, that Missy could almost believe that he was completely better again.

"Can I come over?" Missy asked eagerly. "Will they let me see you?"

Joshua laughed. "I'll get Dad to smuggle you in."

Dad... It sounded strange to hear Joshua address her father that way, but Missy was grateful for the improved relationship between the two of them.

"She's gotta eat her breakfast first!" Charles raised his voice so that Joshua could hear.

Missy rolled her eyes. Joshua laughed and said that she should listen to her elders. "But hurry over as soon as you're done," he added.

Missy had just sat down at the table again when Cynarra appeared in the doorway. She looked tousled and sleepy and incredibly cute.

Missy held her arms out to her. "Hey, baby girl."

With a huge smile, Cynarra walked into her embrace.

"Hey, where's my good morning hug?" Martha asked, pretending to sound aggrieved.

"And where's mine?" Charles echoed.

With a happy giggle, Cynarra gave and received a hug from both Martha and Charles.

"And now, how would you like some yummy blueberry pancakes?" Martha asked, setting a steaming plate down on the table as she spoke.

Missy was anxious to see Joshua and hurried through her meal. Cynarra and Keiron already seemed to be making plans for the day. Missy thanked her grandmother for the pancakes and announced that she was heading over to the Health Center.

Cynarra immediately jumped to her feet. "Can I come, too?"

Missy didn't have the heart to say no. "Sure," she said with a smile.

The little girl was already halfway across the room when Martha said, "Maybe we should just do a little something with your hair first."

Missy noticed that Cynarra's hair did look a little messy.

"Can I have my hair in a pony-tail like Mommy?"

"Sure can, baby girl," Martha said.

The phone rang at that moment. It was Missy's father wanting to know if she could pick up Katherine's bags from the hotel on her way over.

Cynarra was excited about having her hair fixed like Missy's and she commented about the fact that they were both wearing the same color of sweaters, a deep magenta. Missy thought that maybe the two of them should go shopping soon; maybe buy some of those matching mother-daughter outfits.

Missy and Cynarra stopped by Katherine's room first to drop off her bags. Missy wasn't surprised to find her father there, but she was a bit startled to see him sitting on the edge of Katherine's bed, holding her hand. And when he bent to kiss her...

Missy cleared her throat loudly. "Hello..."

It was the glance that passed between the two of them that astonished Missy the most. It was the look that she'd so often seen between her mom and dad!

And the joy on her father's face—that too held a distant memory.

Missy made a quick decision. She had loved her mother very much and no one could or would replace her. But this past winter, it was like she'd lost her father, too. If Katherine could help him, then Missy would gladly support their growing friendship. Her father had grieved long enough.

He stood up quickly and walked toward her, his eyes begging her to understand. "Missy, honey..." he said.

She put her arms around him and squeezed him tight. "I'm so happy for you, Daddy," she said.

"Really?" There was no mistaking the joy in his voice, or in his actions as he picked her up and whirled her around, like a spinning top, laughing all the while.

"My turn! My turn!" Cynarra called out.

Jeff released Missy and picked up Cynarra. "Okay," he said, "But I have to spin you around the other way so I won't get dizzy."

Cynarra giggled and then began to laugh outright as Jeff twirled her around in circles and then collapsed into the chair with her on his lap.

Missy glanced over at Katherine but her eyes, filled with admiration, were on Jeff.

"That was fun," Cynarra exclaimed. "Can we do it again?"

"Not right away!" Jeff gasped, obviously out of breath.

Missy laughed. "I think I wore him out before he even picked you up."

"Can I go see Daddy now?" Cynarra asked, scooting off Jeff's lap and heading towards the door.

Missy threw Katherine and her father a smile before hurrying after Cynarra, who was already running down the hallway.

Joshua looked great! It almost seemed as if he was completely better. But the doctor had warned her that he would have good and bad days, and he still definitely did need open heart surgery—and soon.

Missy put her worried thoughts aside and smiled at her husband and new daughter. Cynarra was chattering away about matching ponytails and sweaters. Joshua grinned up at Missy and proclaimed them to be: "the two most beautiful women in the whole wide world!"

Cynarra told him about the blueberry pancakes they'd had for breakfast and asked Joshua if he'd had breakfast yet.

He smiled at her. "Yep, doesn't sound as good as yours, though."

"You were able to eat something, though?" Missy asked, unable to keep the concern from her voice.

Joshua reached out for her hand. "My throat's getting better now," he assured her. "It's much easier to swallow."

Missy kept hold of Joshua's hand as Cynarra chattered on about how many pancakes she'd had compared to Keiron. Missy and Joshua frequently exchanged loving glances as Cynarra continued to talk about how much further she could throw rocks than Keiron… but he knew how to skip them over the surface of the water and she didn't know how to do that yet...

The time passed quickly. Katherine and Jeff joined them, Jeff pushing the wheelchair with Katherine's injured ankle propped up on one of the footrests.

Jeff made a fresh pot of coffee and served it. The conversation was kept purposely light for Joshua's sake. Jeff brought up the topic of hobbies and everyone started to talk about that.

Katherine said that she really liked reading and Cynarra smiled broadly and said that she liked reading too. Missy was trying to think about what her hobby might be when Katherine squeezed her father's hand and asked, "How about you?"

Jeff shrugged. "I don't know. I've been working on getting in shape..."

Katherine lifted an eyebrow. "Ahh... now the key word there is 'work'. If you have to work at it, that's not a hobby. What is it that you do for relaxation?"

Jeff shook his head. "I'm not sure."

"Okay," Katherine said, "think back to a time when you were really happy..."

Missy felt her heart skip a beat. What if he started thinking about her mom again? Could it drive him into another depression?

But to her surprise, her dad looked first at Cynarra and then over at Missy. "One of the times I best remember is telling stories to my girls," he said softly.

"He is one of the best story-tellers in the whole world," Missy enthused. "Noah's ark is *the* best! Every time he would tell it, there'd be different animals. Of course, the story came complete with *all* the different animal sounds."

Her father smiled contentedly as Missy continued, "Usually there was sound *and* action!"

Cynarra's eyes were open wide and shining. Missy said, "You should get Grandpa to tell you the story about the big storm on the Sea of Galilee."

"Grandpa?" Cynarra turned shining eyes toward him.

Jeff opened his arms to her and Cynarra climbed up onto his lap. "Okay," he said in a deep theatrical voice, "as long as you promise not to be too scared. There's ghosts in this story…"

"Dad!" Missy protested.

"Well, at least they thought it was a ghost," he amended with a wide grin.

Everyone was laughing when suddenly a harsh voice spoke from behind them. "No visitors, eh?"

Missy groaned inwardly. *Yvonne Quill*…

Her instinctive reaction was to move closer to Joshua. She leaned in to him, entwining her arm in his, willing her strength and courage to him.

Cynarra had buried her face in Jeff's shoulder.

"Not an Indian among the lot of you," Yvonne sneered. "Can't be family members."

Missy clung tighter to Joshua. "It's okay," she whispered.

Yvonne took a step inside the room. "You black ones should go back to Africa and you Yankees—"

Suddenly, there were two police officers behind her, filling the doorway. Police Chief Colin Hill cleared his throat. "Excuse me…"

Yvonne turned, gasped in alarm, and pushed her way between the two officers. The door to the outer room slammed shut an instant later.

The other police officer, Keegan Littledeer, glanced back at the closed door and then around at the assembled group. "What was that all about?" he asked.

"Guess she has a guilty conscience," Jeff said.

"Did you want to see me, officers?" Katherine asked.

"Yes, if now would be a good time," Colin answered. "We're a bit earlier than we said we would be."

Katherine smiled. "Now will be fine."

Colin stepped forward holding a large black leather bag. "We found your bag, Ms. Blake-Jones."

"So quickly?"

"Your money's gone," Colin said, "but everything else seems to be intact. Maybe you could check it out."

Even Katherine's camera was still in the bag! Her voice sounded a little dazed as she said, "I would have given them the money. They… seemed so angry… like all they wanted to do was to… hurt me."

Jeff, with a quick glance at Joshua and Cynarra, suggested that they move out of the room. "I'll make some fresh coffee and take it down to you guys," he said.

"We'll stay in here," Missy said, looking at Cynarra as she spoke. "There was something that I wanted to tell you about."

The little girl's eyes lit up with expectation, and Missy said, "Yesterday, Grandma heard the baby's heartbeat!"

JEFF SMILED AT CYNARRA'S WIDE-EYED enthusiasm, gave Joshua a small salute, and offered to push Katherine's wheelchair for her.

Keegan grabbed the two chairs from where Jeff had left them in the hallway the night before, and took them along to Katherine's room.

Colin and Keegan settled into the two chairs. Jeff remained standing behind Katherine's wheelchair, suddenly unsure of his role.

Colin took the lead. "Ms. Blake-Jones," he said in official tones, "do you wish to have Dr. Peters present during this interview?"

Katherine smiled up at Jeff. "Yes," she said softly, reaching for his hand.

Jeff gave her hand a quick squeeze then pulled the bedside chair up close to her wheelchair. He rested his forearm beside hers on the arm of the wheelchair so that they could comfortably hold hands for the duration of the interview.

Colin and Keegan were eyeing him with inquisitive grins, but Jeff simply smiled serenely back at them. When it was time for announcements, he would make them.

"I've been thinking about the descriptions…" Katherine said in a trembling voice.

Jeff leaned closer toward her and held her hand more tightly and Keegan flipped open his notebook as Colin said gently, "Just take your time."

"It was fairly well lit and not too far to walk," Katherine began again, her voice a little steadier now. "I wasn't expecting trouble of any kind. My mind was on other things. I was actually crying so I wasn't really paying attention…"

Her words drove like spikes into Jeff's heart. "I'm sorry," he whispered hoarsely.

She waited until he had raised his eyes again to speak gently and lovingly, "It's okay." She waited a moment longer until he nodded solemnly.

Forgiveness given and received.

Katherine kept her hand securely in Jeff's but looked toward the police officers as she continued. "I don't usually panic…"

Colin's eyebrow rose a little. "Usually?"

"I've been in some very difficult situations in my job—as a war correspondent. I was trying to think why it was so different this time. I think it was because I'd been walking around all day and I thought I was among friends and suddenly, I was alone. Just alone…"

Jeff groaned inwardly. *If he could only turn back the clock!*

"When they attacked, I was so surprised that I forgot about the self-defense I knew. At least at the beginning. And then, I was so sure that someone in the hotel would hear and…" Katherine's voice broke off as tears filled her eyes.

Jeff put his arm around her as Katherine continued unsteadily, "Someone did eventually put their head out the door and yell that the police were on their way. It didn't really seem to deter them at all, not till they heard the sirens."

Katherine took a deep breath and Jeff saw her wince from the wound in her side. "One of them had a knife," he said through gritted teeth.

"It'd be best if she just told it her way," Colin advised.

Katherine smiled with sadness in her eyes at Jeff. "Yes, one of them had a knife." She turned back to Colin. "It had a long blade, maybe eight or nine inches with a sharp point on the end, almost like a hook."

"Fish filet knife," Colin surmised.

"The—the thing that I most remember is their anger. It—it was directed toward me and it was so filled with hate. I—I didn't know any of them and they hated me so much…" Her voice trailed off into a whisper.

"Not you," Colin said, shaking his head. "It's what you represent."

"Their anger is a response to all the hurts they have endured in their lifetime," Keegan said.

"And they were likely all under the influence of drugs," Colin added.

Katherine nodded. "I could see that in their eyes."

"What else did you see?" Colin prodded gently.

"The one who was on top of me…" Katherine began.

"On top of you!" Jeff exploded. He felt as if he'd been running and couldn't catch his breath. "They didn't… They didn't…"

"No," Katherine said in a clear, calm voice, holding his eyes fast with hers. "The police came in time."

Jeff forced himself to relax. Colin was looking at him askance. He didn't want to be asked to leave.

"You were describing one of the perpetrators," Keegan said.

Katherine focused her attention on him as he recorded what she was saying. "He had a buzz cut, but his hair was dry; no gel. He was kind of big compared to the rest. Maybe 230 pounds and five foot ten or so. He had this chain around his neck like a dog collar…"

Colin held up his hand. "That's enough," he said with a sigh.

"You know him?" Jeff asked incredulously.

Colin nodded wearily. "Guess we know most of the kids in the community one way or the other. But some, we know a little better than others…"

"He's been in trouble before?" Katherine asked.

"Yeah." Colin sighed again. "And the others…"

"The others…" Katherine said quietly. "The one with the knife…"

Jeff tightened his grip on her. Katherine patted his arm and continued calmly, "He was tall, slim and wore his hair in a pony-tail. He had a bit of a moustache and a goatee. He had on this long black coat and leather gloves…"

Keegan stopped writing. Colin raised his hand wearily again.

Six of the other eight or more that were in the group, Katherine was able to describe well enough for Keegan and Colin to recognize.

Each time an identification was made, the two men reacted with both resignation and sadness. It was almost as if each boy was a son or a brother to them. Jeff, watching them trudge wearily out of the room, thought about how hard it must be to be a police officer in such a small community.

Katherine looked exhausted, too. Jeff helped her back to bed and checked to see when her next dose of pain medication was due.

He was about to go out to the nurses' station when Katherine spoke his name. She reached out her hand and he took it. "Those boys…" she began.

Jeff sat down in the chair by her bed. "Yes…"

"They're the same ones that Josh is trying to help."

Jeff nodded, wondering if her thoughts were traveling along the same line as his.

They were. "Maybe there's something we can do," Katherine said.

Jeff felt a swell of love for her. "Maybe."

Chapter 11

JEFF WAS SURPRISED TO SEE Jamie come into the room just behind the nurse bringing Katherine's medication. He lifted an eyebrow in her direction. "You really do live here, don't you?"

Jamie laughed. "Actually, I'm on my way to church. I just stopped by to see Amy and I thought I'd see how you guys were doing."

Jeff was distracted by the movement beside him. The nurse had pills for Katherine. *Was she high enough up in the bed? Did she need some water? No, the nurse had a little paper cup of water on the tray with the medication...*

"We're doing fine, thanks," Katherine answered as she accepted the pills and water from the nurse.

Jeff watched her swallow them before turning back to Jamie. She'd said something about church... He hadn't attended much during the past winter. It was just easier not to be around people...

"I guess I should go," he said with his head bowed, the sadness of the past winter heavy in his voice.

"What!" Jamie exclaimed.

"Go?" Katherine's voice trembled.

Jeff glanced quickly from one of them to the other. "To church…"

Katherine smiled tremulously, relief obvious in her eyes. Jamie just shook her head.

"When *do* you have to go, Jeff...?" Katherine asked, adding uncertainly, "...back to where you have to go?"

"The treatment center," Jeff supplied with a fragile smile. He hadn't purposely avoided the topic and obviously someone had already told her all about it, anyway. "I've got a ticket booked for tomorrow morning."

He hadn't meant to speak harshly. He hadn't meant to draw back, to distance himself... But it was what he had done... again.

"Jeff..." Katherine said his name with desperate urgency, her hand extended toward him.

He reached out for her, felt the warmth of her touch and knew that the winter was truly past. Spring, with its promise of new beginnings and new hope, was waiting to embrace him.

Katherine leaned forward, wrapping her arm around him, pulling him closer. "I'm not going to lose you," she whispered.

She sealed the promise of her words with a kiss. Jeff felt as if he were drowning again but this time in a sea of love. And he needed no rescuing.

"Would you like to talk about it?" Katherine asked in a gentle voice a few minutes later.

"It?" Jeff asked, feeling a little bewildered.

Katherine smiled and began in a tentative voice. "I guess one way or the other, I've ended up spending a lot of time with different members of your family. And before you ask..." She raised her hand. "...It wasn't all to do with getting a headline story."

Jeff nodded. "Okay," he said quietly.

Katherine sighed. "I've been trying to sort through my own motives in all of this. In some ways, I guess, I'm here under false pretences…"

Jeff grew steadily more anxious. *What was Katherine trying to say?*

She smiled wanly. "In some ways, I've used my 'press badge' as a shield. I don't need to write up this story. Gabriel had a very good insurance policy and I was advised to immediately invest the principle. Over the years, I have done an article or two. But I don't have to do this one…"

"It's okay if you do," Jeff said cautiously.

Katherine sighed and turned away. "I've been mostly just drifting along since Gabriel died," she said, staring at the wall ahead of her. "My son keeps me focused on life and living. I cook and eat nutritious food because I'm making it for him, too. I stay active because I know that's what's good for him, too. We go swimming and hiking and to theme parks and we usually have a whole raft of his friends along with us. And we get together with other families who have kids."

Jeff took her hand and gently touched the side of her cheek. She turned toward him as she continued. "My mom has been great, too. She's such an awesome grandma. Patrick hardly notices when I'm gone. I called him yesterday and he could hardly wait to get off the phone. They were heading to the zoo."

"Your mom lives with you?" Jeff asked.

Katherine smiled wanly. "Actually, I guess you could say that we live with her. When my dad got so ill, she asked if I could come and help. I sold our house and moved in with them. It was what I needed to do. I'd been clinging to the past and the move forced me to sort through Gabriel's belongings and pack some of them away and sell some of them."

Jeff remembered how hard it had been for him to do that with Jenny's stuff. But once he'd made the decision to move, his sister, Coralee, and her husband had come and done most of the work for him. In retrospect, Jeff realized that he should have waited a bit longer before selling the house, quitting his job and moving away. He'd done everything in a haze of grief and despair.

"...Rachel's Children was the pinnacle of his career."

Jeff snapped his attention back to Katherine. She smiled forgivingly and repeated the words that he had missed. "My father and I talked a lot."

Jeff nodded as Katherine continued. "During the last few months, he got so weak, he spent most of the day in bed. And I would sit with him. He loved to talk about the old days. He'd spent some time up here, following the story while Rachel's Children was being dismantled and I think he kept in touch a bit with what's been happening in the intervening years."

"The children's camp..." Jeff suggested.

"That," Katherine agreed, "and the laws regarding use of fetal tissue for research and organ transplant."

Jeff nodded solemnly.

"He never gave up the fight," Katherine said. "Two weeks before he died, he dictated a letter to the editor on the subject of partial birth abortions."

Katherine smiled nostalgically. "But his favorite topic was always Rachel's Children, the work at Goldrock Lodge, and the people of Rabbit Lake. I guess that's part of the reason why, after he passed away, I wanted to come up here."

Jeff leaned toward her and planted a kiss on her lips. "It doesn't matter why you came her," he said affectionately. "I'm just glad you're here."

"But you asked me… last night."

Jeff groaned. "I wish I could undo every single thing I said."

"It was a fair question," Katherine protested weakly.

"No, it wasn't," Jeff insisted. "You have every right to come here and visit whomever you wish and talk about whatever they and you want to talk about."

"It seemed natural that we talk about you," Katherine said shyly.

Jeff grinned. "It did?"

"I was talking to your mom and your daughter and your son-in-law…"

Jeff raised an eyebrow. "All about me?" he teased.

Katherine punched him playfully in the arm. "Not *all* about you." Her voice suddenly grew serious as she continued, "They did mention that you were at a treatment center because you'd been misusing prescription medications."

Jeff's jaw tightened. "…That I'd stolen from this very building that we're in right now."

"Yes, I knew that," Katherine said in a quiet voice.

She had a tight grip on his hand. Jeff smiled ruefully. She wasn't about to let him go any time soon.

"We've all done things we regret," she said gently. "and the treatment center has helped…"

Jeff nodded. "Yeah, it's helped a lot. The arrest was really a blessing. I'm glad that someone finally had the courage to confront me. I think I had convinced myself that no one else knew or even suspected."

Katherine relaxed her hold on his hand a bit but didn't let go. "How much longer do you have?" she asked.

"I have an assessment coming up on Tuesday," Jeff said. "They'll likely be able to give me a projected release date by then."

"Will it be... like months or...?" she asked anxiously.

"No," Jeff assured her, "We're talking days or weeks."

The relief on her face was so obvious, Jeff had to smile. "You have plans?"

Katherine's voice was a little slurred. "Nothing definite."

The pain medication must have started taking effect. Her eyelids were drooping. "Maybe we can talk about it when you wake up," Jeff suggested.

"Okay," Katherine mumbled as she closed her eyes.

Jeff held her hand until he was sure that she was asleep, then he gently released it and settled back into a more comfortable position on the chair.

As he watched her, Jeff couldn't help thinking about all the times he'd sat at Jenny's bedside. It had been the worst agony imaginable to watch her slowly and painfully slip further and further away from him until she was completely gone to a place where he could no longer reach her. He had selfishly clung to her until she had begged him to let her go, to release her from this world to the next. Somehow, he must have convinced her that he was at peace, for she had slipped away one day with a faint smile on her lips. But he hadn't been at peace. He'd been in torment, fighting against the injustice and cruelty of her death every step of the way. Jeff knew that his anger had been directed at God. He had reversed the anger into a severe depression. He had shut out friends and family that had sought to comfort him. And he had shut out God.

Over the months, he had withdrawn further and further, using drugs to insulate and isolate himself from everyone around him.

None of his family or friends in the community had had the courage to confront him about his growing addiction. They had finally resorted to outside help from the RCMP, not realizing that the RCMP would send young Andrew back to his home community to "discover" who was stealing drugs from the Health Center. Jeff very much regretted all the pain that had been caused to Andrew and to Jasmine through the events surrounding his arrest.

Going through detox had cleared his mind. The pain was still there, but Jeff was determined now to face life with courage and to accept the support offered by his family, his friends and most of all his Best Friend, the Lord Jesus.

"She sleeping?"

Jamie's words, though quietly spoken, startled Jeff; he'd been so deep in thought. He nodded toward her and rose quickly to his feet.

Jamie followed him into the hallway, where Jeff asked, "Weren't you on your way to church?"

Jamie laughed. "I've gone and come back. Did you miss me?"

"Uh—no," Jeff stammered. He hadn't even noticed her leaving.

Jamie laughed again and punched him lightly in the shoulder. "Bet you'd notice if Katherine left the room."

Jeff shook his head and grinned. "Yeah, probably," he admitted.

"I think they're planning to release her later today," Jamie said.

Jeff nodded as Jamie continued, "She's welcome to stay at our house, if she doesn't mind sharing a room with Kaitlyn. It might be nicer for her instead of staying at a hotel."

Jeff smiled. "Thanks. I'll ask her when she wakes up."

There was a flurry of movement and Jeff turned to see Cynarra burst into the room. "Grandpa, I went to Sunday School!"

Jeff grinned. "That's great. How did you like it?"

"We played games and had stories and sang songs. It was fun!"

Jeff smiled at his mother who was standing with Charles and Keiron.

"Can we go visit my daddy?" Cynarra asked.

"Maybe I'll just go check to see how he's doing?" Jeff said.

They followed him down the hallway but waited outside as Jeff went in to Joshua's room.

As soon as he walked in, Jeff could hear the gentle strumming of a guitar. He smiled as he saw Missy looking starry-eyed and content as she watched Joshua sitting up in a chair with his guitar.

"Sounds good," Jeff said.

Joshua grinned up at him. "It's been a while."

Missy turned and smiled broadly at her father. "I was thinking about what you said about hobbies and I remembered how Joshua used to always like to play the guitar."

"So, how are you feeling?" Jeff asked his son-in-law.

"Relaxed. Content," Joshua answered.

"Up to visitors?" Jeff queried.

"Sure," Joshua said with a grin.

Jeff ushered Martha, Charles, Keiron and Cynarra into the room. Cynarra immediately began regaling Joshua with stories about her Sunday School experience. She noticed his guitar and asked if he knew any of the songs she'd heard that morning. Joshua admitted that he did and a few minutes later, she had the whole room singing along with her, one song after another.

Dr. Smith walked in as they were singing and stood watching with a smile on his face as they wound up a rousing rendition of the song, "Mercy is Falling."

He glanced at the monitors and pulled out his prescription pad, scribbled a note, tore off a sheet and handed it to Joshua.

Joshua read it and laughed as he passed it around for everyone else to see. Jeff read: "15 minutes of group singing, twice a day, or as needed."

Missy asked Dr. Smith, "Can Joshua go home today?"

Jeff was a little surprised when the younger doctor shook his head. "We'll get you up and walking around the room a bit," he said. "But I'd rather speak to Dr. Phillips before discharging you. We need to discuss a date for your operation, too. I'll likely be speaking to him tomorrow morning."

The mood in the room grew decidedly more somber, especially after the mention of Joshua's imminent operation. But Joshua was not about to let that last too long. With a twinkle in his eye he asked, "So how about the song, 'We will dance'?"

Dr. Smith slipped out of the room and Jeff followed him, as the happy sounds of singing began again behind them.

Jeff asked if Katherine would be discharged soon.

"She can go home whenever she's ready," Dr. Smith said. "Just no heavy lifting for a few days. She shouldn't vacuum and—"

Something in Jeff's manner must have registered for the younger doctor stopped abruptly.

"We're not... I'm not..." Jeff stumbled.

"Right," Dr. Smith spoke briskly. "So you're saying she lives alone?"

"No," Jeff said, running his fingers through his hair. "No, that's not what I'm saying. She's from out of town. She's a visitor... staying at the hotel."

Dr. Smith said, "Well, in any case, she can be discharged today. The nurse can arrange for some crutches for her to use for a day or two. I'll want to check the stitches before she goes, and she should see her own doctor in a week or two."

They'd arrived at Katherine's room and went in together. She was still asleep. "Better let her rest," Dr. Smith advised. "I'll come back later."

He started out the door but stopped when he realized that Jeff was not with him. Dr. Smith glanced back curiously.

"I'll... um... just wait for her to wake up," Jeff said, moving further into the room instead of out of it.

He sat down in a chair by the bed and thought of his relationship with Katherine. He cared very deeply for her and it was obvious that she felt something for him as well, but nothing had been spoken aloud.

And what was their relationship? It was too soon to make any long-term commitment, although Jeff could not, for a moment, imagine living the rest of his life without her. They were certainly more than just friends...

Jeff glanced up at that moment and found Katherine smiling at him.

Jeff felt his heart do little flip-flops. Definitely more than just friends...

"Would you... uh... like to go on a date?" he asked.

Katherine laughed merrily. "Where did you have in mind? The Riverview Restaurant in New York City or maybe the Ivory Palace in Chicago?"

Jeff grinned and raised an eyebrow. "I was thinking somewhere a bit closer…"

Katherine gave him a huge smile. "There's a coffee shop at the hotel. They make great coffee and excellent pie."

"Would you like to go out for dinner with me tonight?" Jeff asked. "Dr. Smith said that you could be discharged as soon as you feel ready."

"Well, I'm feeling pretty good right now," Katherine said. "And I'd love to go out on a date with you tonight."

Katherine gratefully accepted Jamie's invitation to stay with her family and when she was dressed and ready to go, Jeff drove her over there.

She'd already met Jamie's husband, Bill, and their children, Kaitlyn and Andrew, while she had been visiting Jasmine and the babies with Martha. Everyone made her feel right at home.

Jeff and Katherine went out for dinner at the hotel restaurant, ordering the special for the day—fresh pickerel with mashed potatoes and cream style corn. Betty had made apple pie that morning and they both had a piece—a la mode. They lingered over coffee and finally left three hours after they had arrived!

Jeff hadn't wanted the evening to end, but he could tell that Katherine was getting tired. She was still taking some pain medication as well, which was also adding to her drowsiness.

He drove her back to the Martins, where they lingered a bit over their farewells, then Jeff returned to the family suite at the Health Center to spend his final night before going back to serve his remaining sentence at the treatment facility.

Chapter 12

JEFF HAD TOLD KATHERINE THAT he expected the assessment to go well, but he was surprised when he was given a conditional release that very day! He was required to call in every day for the first week and then once a week for the following month, as sort of a probation period.

Jeff called Katherine first with the news and then Missy. He was happy to hear that Joshua had been released from the hospital. He called Jasmine, and was pleased with her report as well. Amy was having her first night at home. Jasmine had a lot of support with family and friends providing meals and helping with the babies. And there was enough medical know-how with Jamie's and Martha's frequent visits.

Missy had offered to meet him at the airport, but so had Katherine. And Jamie had invited him to eat supper with them. Jeff told Missy he would get to the lodge by eight o'clock at the latest, and eagerly accepted Jamie's invitation to supper. "We have lots of food," she said. "I made two casseroles: one for Andrew to take over to Jasmine's, and one for ourselves. But Kaitlyn is going over to help with the babies, too, so there will just be Bill and I, and the two of you."

Though it had only been hours, it felt as if it had been days or weeks since he'd seen Katherine. Jeff felt like a grinning fool, barely able to keep up with the conversation around the table and totally unable to stop smiling.

He would have liked some time alone with Katherine, but she was planning to stay for a couple more days, so they would have time. She said that she'd told her mom about the attack but hadn't wanted to alarm her seven-year-old son, Patrick. The knife wound was healing quite well, and her ankle had just been twisted a little, not sprained, and she was managing without crutches for the most part.

"Jamie keeps badgering me to rest," Katherine complained, "but I'm feeling fine."

She was smiling as she said it, and Jeff was pleased that Katherine was getting to know two of his oldest and best friends.

"Well," Jamie spoke in defense, "she always wants to help me. Now, does it look like I need help?"

Jeff grinned as she waved her arms around her gloriously messy house, and Bill winked and said, "Don't answer that!"

Jamie punched him in the arm and said her favorite Phyllis Diller quote: "Cleaning the house while the kids are still growing is like shoveling the walk while it's still snowing!"

Bill raised an eyebrow. "Kaitlyn's almost grown. Then what are you gonna do?"

Jamie shrugged. "Find a new saying, I guess."

The time sped by, and it was half past seven before he knew it. Jeff wanted to stop by quick to see Jasmine and the babies, and he had promised to be at the lodge by eight.

It was hard to say goodbye to Katherine but not as hard as it had been that morning when they'd had no idea when they'd see each other again.

Bill dropped Jeff off at the house on Sandy Point, picking up Andrew at the same time. Kaitlyn was planning to spend the night, as was Martha.

Jeff was pleased with his granddaughters' progress. And he was happy to see all the support that Jasmine had. Besides Andrew, Kaitlyn, and Martha, Charles was also there. Bill lingered a while, and Jeff spent a few moments visiting with them all before heading up to lodge.

Coming out to the main road, he was surprised to see Yvonne Quill striding in the opposite direction away from the lodge, her hand fastened onto the back of Keiron's neck as she pushed him ahead of her.

Jeff stood irresolute for a moment, wondering if there was anything he could do to help Keiron, before resuming his walk to the lodge, picking up the pace as his anxiety rose. If Yvonne had forcibly taken Keiron…

He walked in without knocking and quickly saw that his concern had been warranted.

Joshua was sitting close to the door, his elbows on a table, his bowed head resting in his hands, his posture one of abject defeat.

Missy was standing glaring at him, her arms folded in front of her.

Cynarra was over by a window watching as Keiron disappeared down the road. She turned toward Jeff, and he could see huge tears running down her cheeks.

"What happened, Josh?" Jeff asked.

Missy spoke through gritted teeth, "Yvonne Quill happened. That's what happened."

Cynarra ran towards Jeff. "She took him, Grandpa. She just took him!"

Jeff knelt down and hugged her as she wept. He glanced up at Missy. Her arms were no longer folded. She looked more sad than angry.

"Maybe you could make us some tea, honey," Jeff said to her. "Do you think you could help, Cynarra?"

As Missy and Cynarra headed toward the kitchen, Jeff gently took Joshua's arm. "Let's go sit somewhere more comfortable," he said.

They made their way to the south end of the lodge where Jeff led Joshua to the big recliner while he lit a fire in the great stone fireplace.

After the fire was going well, Jeff settled into the sofa adjacent from his son-in-law.

"Josh…" Jeff prompted.

Joshua turned bleak eyes toward him and said in a hoarse voice, "She's my aunt."

Jeff quelled the anger that threatened to spill over into angry words and instead replied in a calm voice, "You've said that before."

"She took care of me and my sister for almost five years while our father was in prison."

"You feel you owe her something…"

Joshua shook his head. "You don't understand! She's my auntie."

"No, I don't understand," Jeff said, the image of Missy and the children fresh in his mind. "I think you need to explain it to me."

Joshua raised his chin. "If you were Ojibway…"

Jeff stood abruptly to his feet and pulled out his cell phone. Charles might still be at Jasmine's.

In the end, Jeff invited both his mom and Charles to come over. Missy and Cynarra could perhaps use Martha's kind words and wise counsel. He didn't explain much to Charles and Martha—just told them that they were needed.

They hurried over and both arrived breathless. Jeff asked his mother to check on Missy, and invited Charles to join him by the fire.

Charles, seeing Joshua's demeanor, put a comforting hand on his shoulder before sitting down in the spot that Jeff had vacated.

Jeff grabbed a straight-backed dining room chair and sat down opposite them.

Charles looked inquiringly at Joshua, but allowed Jeff to speak first.

Forcing himself to remain calm, Jeff said, "Perhaps you can explain to me why Joshua feels obliged to invite his aunt to verbally and physically abuse my daughter and grandchildren."

Joshua raised his voice in protest. "I don't!"

Jeff turned toward him. "You do nothing to stop her."

"I—I—don't," Joshua stuttered. "Not—not physical abuse…"

Though he wished he didn't have to, Jeff knew that he had to push the issue. "Who locked Missy in the decline?" he demanded. "Who kidnapped Cynarra? Why is Missy angry and why was Cynarra crying? Why did you allow Yvonne to take Keiron back again?"

Joshua didn't answer but bowed his head once more.

Jeff couldn't keep the challenge out of his voice as he turned to Charles. "He said I might understand if I was Ojibway."

Charles nodded solemnly but took a moment to frame a reply.

"Perhaps," he finally said, "we could pray."

Jeff couldn't disagree. They did need divine wisdom and guidance.

Charles prayed, asking God not only for wisdom but for courage and strength to do His will.

After Charles finished praying, he said in a sad, quiet voice. "It's my fault."

Joshua protested. "No!"

But Charles nodded. "Yes, it is," he said. "I've been seeing this going on for years and never did anything about it. I guess… I guess I was a bit afraid of Yvonne myself."

Joshua was about to protest further, but Charles put up his hand and shook his head. "I guess none of us enjoys confrontation but sometimes, that's what needs to happen."

Jeff felt a wave of relief and a good deal of admiration for the older man. "What would you advise us to do?" he asked.

Charles's reply shocked him. "We need to call the police."

"No!" Joshua cried out.

Charles sighed heavily. "Yes," he said, "and the sooner the better."

Jeff rose to get the phone, but Charles intercepted him. "I'll call," he said.

It was Colin who arrived a few moments later.

Missy was just coming out of the kitchen with some tea and cookies, Martha and Cynarra helping her to carry them over to the sitting area by the fire.

She heard her father greet Colin, and as they crossed the floor, heard Colin ask, "What's up?"

"Yvonne Quill," Jeff replied succinctly.

Colin asked in a weary voice, "What's she done now?"

Missy answered, "It's not just what she's done now but what she's been doing all of Joshua's life!"

Colin eased down into a chair, glanced around at the others, then focused on Joshua, still seated in the recliner. "Josh?"

Joshua slowly raised his head, his eyes bleak with despair. "She speaks kind of rough some times…"

Missy interjected, "It's verbal abuse, Joshua. That's what it is."

Colin's eyes traveled slowly back to meet hers. "So what exactly do you want me to do?"

Missy's voice trembled with anger. "I want you to arrest her—put a restraining order against her—do something!"

Colin's voice remained calm. "It isn't against the law for one person to speak unkindly toward another, especially if both parties are adults and one is not in a position of control over another, as it would be in the case of a caregiver or employer or spouse. If there have been no actual physical threats…"

Missy didn't hear the rest as she sank wearily back down onto the couch. *It isn't against the law.* There was no law against viciously stabbing and hacking away at a person's self-worth until there remained nothing but a crumbled heap of insecurities! No law against destroying a man's spirit to the point where it also destroyed his body! No law against killing a marriage, a family, and a ministry…

"She could be charged with kidnapping and attempted murder," her father said.

Missy shook her head. "She's never done that. It's her words that are destroying us—"

"She did it to you," her father said. "We should have reported it to the police right away. And she took Cynarra against her will."

"She's her great-aunt," Joshua protested.

Missy jumped to her feet again. "You always defend her!" she yelled.

Colin cleared his throat. "Can we maybe back up a bit? Jeff, what is this about kidnapping and attempted murder?"

"It's nothing," Missy said dismissively. "That old witch can't hurt me."

"But you were hurt," her father insisted. "If we hadn't found you—"

"The reason no one found me is because no one was looking! And no one was looking because Yvonne had convinced my husband that I had left him."

Colin stood to his feet. "If you're not willing to press charges…"

Missy sank back onto the couch again. "What good would it do? No one is going to throw an old woman in jail—and that's the only thing that would keep her away from us."

"No, we are going to press charges," Jeff insisted. "And these are very serious charges of attempted murder and kidnapping."

Colin's demeanor changed immediately. He flipped his notebook open, sat down again, and motioned for Jeff to pull up a chair close to him.

"I want to hear everything—from the beginning."

Jeff began by saying that Yvonne had knocked Missy unconscious and locked her in the decline.

Colin immediately pulled out his phone. "I'll want another officer to be present," he said. "Someone to take notes."

"And she took Keiron!" Cynarra cried out. "And she always hits him and says mean things to him."

"You saw her hitting him?" Colin asked gravely.

"She hit me, too—but she hits Keiron all the time."

Colin looked thoughtful for a moment, and when he got through to the station, he asked that, in addition to another police officer, they also arrange for a social worker to come and join them.

THE OFFICER WAS A YOUNG woman whom Missy had not met, who introduced herself as Officer Mullins. The social worker, Frank Keesick, was a local man whom Missy had known for years.

Their story came out bit by bit. Missy was questioned and then Cynarra, and finally Joshua.

Frank was of the opinion that it would be better for Keiron to be cared for by Joshua and his wife. Even if Yvonne's arrest was not imminent, and her care of Keiron in question, Joshua was a nearer relative and was well able to supply for the boy's needs.

Frank listened as Missy described how Yvonne had knocked her unconscious and locked her in the decline, and as Cynarra told of her experience being kidnapped by Yvonne.

"I'd like to get Keiron out of there as soon as possible," he said. "When were you going to make the arrest, Colin?"

Colin glanced at his watch. "Right away."

Missy looked at her watch also—9:45.

"You can take Keiron right now?" Frank asked her.

"Yes, of course!" Missy replied. "He stayed here last night. We have a room ready for him—if you'd like to see it…"

Frank smiled. "I'm sure it's fine."

Joshua stood to his feet. "I want to go with you," he said.

"No!" Missy exclaimed.

Cynarra jumped up. "Me, too!"

Missy was appalled. "No, Cynarra—and that's final."

Cynarra subsided back onto the sofa but Joshua remained standing. "I have to go," he said calmly. "I shouldn't have let her take him."

Frank nodded solemnly, and to Missy's surprise neither her father nor Charles tried to talk Joshua out of going—and neither volunteered to go with him!

"I'd go with you," her father said, "but it sounds as if there is going to be quite a large group of you already."

"We'll be right back," Frank promised.

MISSY FUSSED A BIT, MAKING sure that Joshua had a coat, and Jeff actually took his pulse! Both told him to be careful. And Cynarra gave him a big, tearful hug.

Colin and Officer Mullins rode in the cruiser, and Joshua went with Frank.

They arrived together but the three men held back a little as Officer Mullins knocked on the door.

Yvonne was still fully clothed and didn't appear to have been sleeping yet.

"Yvonne Quill?" Officer Mullins confirmed.

Yvonne peered into the darkness at the others. "Who wants to know?"

Colin stepped forward. "Yvonne Quill, you are under arrest for attempted murder and kidnapping."

Yvonne sneered at him and held out her hands to be cuffed. "Go ahead," she said. "The charges will never stick. There were no witnesses. It'll be her word against mine."

Joshua slid past her, anxious to get to Keiron.

She spun around and let loose the usual vitriol of abuse, but for once, the words had no effect on him. Joshua didn't even slow down, his concern for Keiron taking precedence over any current drama his aunt wanted to draw him into.

There were two bedrooms in the house; one that was exclusively for his aunt, and the other room where other family members slept.

A single bulb dimly lit the narrow hallway. Joshua hurried past his aunt's room to the one further down. The door was shut. Joshua knocked, and then turned the knob, but the door held fast. He heard the sound of metal against metal, and looked up to see a hook and eye lock mechanism near the top of the door—Keiron had been locked in!

Joshua's stomach constricted. He felt as if he might throw up —or cry.

His hand trembled as reached towards the lock.

What was he afraid of?

Images flashed through his mind. There had been other doors that he had opened that had caused him great pain. He vividly recalled opening his sister's bedroom door to find that she had taken her own life.

But it was this door—this door and this lock—that were creating the feeling of panic.

In an instant, Joshua remembered the times when he had been locked into this very same room—by Yvonne.

He had huddled in the darkness, afraid to even attempt to open the door, knowing that if she heard him, he would be in for another tongue-lashing and more often than not, a beating as well.

As he flipped open the lock, something unlocked in Joshua's spirit.

He opened the door, felt for the light switch, noted without surprise that the light didn't work, and stepped into the darkness.

"Keiron..." he managed in a trembling voice. "Keiron!" he cried more urgently.

He heard footsteps in the hall, and turned to see Jeff, looking a little sheepish. "Decided I didn't want to let you come here alone, after all," he said.

"I need a flashlight," Joshua said. "Colin might have one."

Jeff nodded and turned back toward the front of the house.

Joshua's eyes were getting accustomed to the dark, and there was a bit of light coming in from the hallway. He could make out the rough outline of the window, boarded up with a piece of plywood. The room was eight foot by ten, and sparsely furnished with a double mattress on the floor and an old dresser with two of its four drawers missing.

Jeff came walking fast down the short hallway with the flashlight in his outstretched hand.

Joshua accepted it with thanks, and shone it all around before striding across the room to pull back the sagging accordion door of the closet.

There were no clothes hanging inside, just a little boy huddled, shivering in the corner with his head bowed.

Joshua fell to his knees, his heart broken. "Keiron…"

Jeff picked up the flashlight that Joshua had dropped and grabbed a blanket off the floor. "Let's get him out of here."

But Joshua felt incapable of moving. "Keiron," he said, tears choking his voice. "I'm sorry. I'm so sorry."

He looked up then, his little face pinched with fear and sadness.

"I shouldn't have let her take you," Joshua said, feeling his eyes fill with tears. "I won't let it happen ever again. I promise."

A tiny spark of hope flared in Keiron's eyes.

Suddenly, they heard Yvonne screaming, "Get your hands off me! I won't go! I won't go! Joshua, help me! Joshua!"

Keiron flew into Joshua's arms, and they held on tight to each other as the screaming increased in volume and intensity.

Jeff hovered close by, his hand on Joshua's shoulder.

They heard the front door slam shut, and the sudden silence was deafening.

Then there was the sound of a man's footsteps walking down the hall.

Joshua turned to see Frank Keesick standing framed in the doorway.

"She's gone," he said, sounding a little shaken.

"Time for us to go, too," Jeff said gently.

Keiron clung to him even tighter, and Joshua looked doubtfully up at his father-in-law. "Maybe just give us a minute."

Jeff bent down, stroked the little boy's hair, and patted his back. "Keiron…" he said softly. "Let me just carry you out to the car, and then you can sit real close to Joshua. Missy and Cynarra are real anxious to see you."

"I—I can walk," Keiron said in a trembling voice.

"Maybe I just need a hug, too," Jeff said.

Keiron released his hold on Joshua and put his arms around Jeff's neck.

As Joshua stood to his feet, Jeff lifted Keiron up and tucked the blanket around him.

The two men turned to see Frank, who had been quietly watching them.

"I'll take good care of him," Joshua promised.

Frank said to Jeff, "You can drive them home if you like." He turned to Joshua. "I'll stop by tomorrow—see how you all are doing."

Chapter 13

Keiron fell asleep on the way back to the lodge, and Jeff carried him in.

Missy, Cynarra, Martha and Charles all rushed to greet them but quieted as they saw that Keiron was asleep.

Jeff carried him up the stairs, Missy following behind him.

Keiron woke up as Jeff laid him down on the Queen-sized bed in the room where Joshua and Missy had slept before Joshua's heart attack.

The little boy's eyes widened as he stared up at Jeff, and terror filled his eyes when Jeff said, "Here, let me help you get undressed."

"Oh, he can do that himself, Dad," Missy said from behind him.

The fear melted from Keiron's eyes and Jeff stumbled backwards, reeling with the shock of what had just transpired.

It made sense, but it was just so hard for Jeff to take in.

He knew that Joshua had been sexually abused as a small child by his older brothers. These older brothers were Keiron's uncles…

As Jeff fled from the room, he felt sick to his stomach. Keiron was only seven years old!

White hot anger shot through him, and for a moment Jeff was paralyzed by it. Then he heard Missy say behind him, "If you're awake, why don't you just come downstairs for a bit? We'll have some cookies and hot chocolate."

In an instant, Jeff quelled the anger, and forced a smile for Missy and Keiron as they emerged from the bedroom.

"I'll be down in a minute to join you," he said, making an effort to keep his voice steady.

As Missy and Keiron started down the stairs, Cynarra noticed them and alerted everyone, and a happy swarm rose to meet them.

Jeff looked down on them, feeling a bit detached. How could this have happened? Who was responsible? How much did the social worker know? He had been pretty quick to get Keiron away from Yvonne. Did Joshua know? Did Joshua suspect? He'd at least known that Keiron was suffering verbal abuse and physical abuse and neglect. Why had he let Keiron remain at Yvonne's house all these years? Was everyone so afraid of her? Even Charles had admitted to that...

"Think I'll head on home," he heard the older man say.

"And I told Jasmine I'd spend the night with her," Martha said.

Missy gave her grandmother a hug. "See you tomorrow," she said.

Cynarra and Keiron were sitting on Joshua's lap in the big recliner by the fireplace. Joshua was reading a book to them.

Everyone seemed to have forgotten Jeff, and it was just as well. He wasn't sure if he could be sociable at the moment.

He would need to talk to Joshua and Missy about his observations of Keiron. Maybe he was wrong—but he didn't think so...

It was late, and it had been a taxing day for Joshua. Jeff decided that he would wait until the following day to confront them.

Missy

With the decision made, he was able to walk over and sit with Missy who had joined Joshua and the children.

Missy had a beautiful, peaceful smile on her face as she gazed fondly over at them.

Keiron's eyes were closed but Cynarra was following along in the book, reading each word as Joshua spoke it aloud.

"He's asleep again," Missy said softly. "Would you mind carrying him upstairs again, Dad? I think he might stay asleep this time."

Jeff shuddered inwardly. He didn't want to see the terror in the little boy's eyes again if he woke up in Jeff's arms, or with Jeff hovering over his bed.

Joshua had stopped reading and was looking lovingly down at Keiron as a father might.

"Dad?" Missy asked into the silence.

Jeff swallowed hard and rose to his feet. He avoided Joshua's eyes, not wanting to add to the young man's stress by introducing a new problem.

He eased Keiron off Joshua's lap and gently lifted him up.

Jeff kept his attention focused on Keiron's face, and wasn't surprised to see the boy's eyes open when they were half-way up the stairs.

"It's okay," he said softly.

By the time they reached the bedroom, Keiron's body was stiff with tension, and when Jeff set him down on the bed, Keiron sprang away, huddling against the headboard, his eyes wide with fear.

Jeff didn't know if it would help at all but he pulled up a chair, thinking that at least he would be more at the boy's level, not looming like some monster high above him.

"Keiron," he began in a voice that shook with emotion, "I am not going to hurt you. There is one thing that you can depend on. I will never ever hurt you."

Keiron remained where he was, his arms wrapped tightly around his chest, warily eyeing Jeff and his every move.

"Another thing you can depend on—Joshua will never ever hurt you. I know him." Jeff took a deep breath and continued, "You're safe here. You can go to sleep and know that no one will hurt you. I'm going to go around and lock all of the doors. You're going to be safe here."

"Is—is my auntie in jail?" Keiron asked in a timid voice.

Jeff was so relieved that Keiron was talking to him that for a moment he was unable himself to speak. He nodded, swallowing past the lump in his throat.

He stood to his feet. "Would you like Missy to come up and say goodnight to you?"

Keiron shook his head and scooted under the blankets.

Missy had left the overhead light on in the room. Jeff turned on a smaller bedside lamp and clicked off the bigger light. "Would you like the door left opened or closed," Jeff asked.

"Closed," came the quiet reply.

Jeff closed the door and headed through his parent's old bedroom and down the stairs intent on fulfilling his promise of locking all the doors, beginning with those in the garage. He went into Missy and Joshua's current bedroom, made sure the patio door was locked, checked the entrance on the south side of the lodge, and then crossed over to the north end of the lodge, locking the patio door there, and finally the front door.

Missy was standing, watching him curiously as he approached. "Just making sure everything's secure," he said.

"I've got fresh sheets on the bed in the first cabin," Missy said. "The one where Rosalee and Michael were staying."

Jeff heard the sadness in her voice as she said the names of the two co-workers who had left the youth program with unresolved bad feelings. He glanced over at Joshua, finishing up the story with Cynarra, and determined again that he wouldn't discuss any more problems with Joshua tonight.

"You guys have a good sleep," he said. "I'll see you in the morning."

JOSHUA WAS SURPRISED WHEN HIS father-in-law called them at seven the next morning. He heard Missy sleepily answering the phone. She came back to bed a few minutes later. "Dad said there wasn't any coffee in the cabin. I unlocked the front door for him. Said he could make himself at home."

Joshua gave her a kiss. "Go back to sleep," he said.

He got dressed and went out to the kitchen to make a pot of coffee.

A few moments later, he heard the front door open and then Jeff appeared in the kitchen doorway, a pen and notebook in his hand.

Joshua poured two cups of coffee. "Good morning!"

"Did you sleep well?" Jeff asked.

"I did," Joshua said, feeling a bit surprised at how well he'd slept. He had felt remarkably calm after his brief encounter with Yvonne the night before. Maybe there was some comfort in the fact that she was in jail.

"Good. We need to talk," Jeff said in a grave voice.

"Okay," Joshua answered cautiously.

They headed over to the south end of the lodge by the fireplace.

Jeff took a sip of coffee and then set it down. "Josh, there's something I need to talk to you about, but first, we need to talk about Yvonne."

"Okay…"

"What are you going to do about her?"

Joshua was surprised at the question. "I thought we already did something—last night. She was arrested. You were there. You heard."

Jeff sighed. "You're hoping that will accomplish something?"

"Yes, of course! At the very least, it will keep her away from all of us for a little while."

"Any idea how long?"

"I—I don't know," Joshua sputtered. "Months…years maybe…"

"If she managed to get hold of a good lawyer last night, she could be released on her own recognizance. She wouldn't be considered a flight risk. The charges are quite serious but the evidence is weak. Missy couldn't even remember who hit her at first. Cynarra would have to testify—or Keiron."

The images of Cynarra or Keiron in a courtroom loomed large in Joshua's mind.

Jeff leaned forward. "They may put some travel restrictions on her—maybe that she doesn't leave the community until after the trial."

"So you're saying…"

"I'm saying that she could walk through that door at any moment."

Joshua's eyes skittered towards the door.

"It's locked," Jeff said.

Joshua felt relieved.

"You can't keep it locked every moment of every day."

Joshua shook his head. "She'd be so angry!"

Jeff sighed. "Joshua," he said kindly, "You have to communicate to her that what she has been doing is not acceptable behavior."

Joshua grimaced. "Yeah, right."

"Josh, you need to do this for yourself and for your family."

"You don't understand," Joshua spoke with some bitterness.

"I think I do understand," Jeff said gently. "I know that confrontation is difficult—but it can be done."

"You don't know my aunt!"

Jeff raised a hand to stem further protests, and began again. "You've heard of 'victim impact statements' right? I'd like you to write one."

"To be read in court?"

"No, that would not be your goal right now. This would be just for you. And possibly to read out loud to Yvonne at the appropriate time."

"She wouldn't listen."

"It doesn't matter, Josh. What matters is that you write it."

Jeff handed him the notebook. "I want you to write a page and then read it to me."

Joshua took the book and set it down on the end table beside his chair.

"Now, Josh."

"What's the rush?" Joshua said, glancing nervously up at his father-in-law.

"I think Keiron has been sexually abused."

Joshua felt like someone had hit him hard in the stomach. He felt out of breath, dizzy, and sick. "No!" he gasped. "He's— he's so young."

"How young were you?" Jeff asked in a gentle voice.

He'd been younger. But Keiron... Why hadn't he known? Why hadn't he done something? He was Keiron's uncle...

"I did some research," Jeff continued. "The most common age for boys to be victims of family-related sexual assault is between ages three and nine."

Joshua picked up the notebook with trembling fingers. "What do you want me to do?" he asked.

"I want you to write down the abusive things that your aunt did to you and what affect that has had on your life."

Joshua took a deep breath. "I—I don't know where to begin."

"Okay," Jeff said, "just tell me about one thing that your aunt did to you that you know for sure is wrong."

Images flashed through Joshua's mind, images he had tried unsuccessfully to erase. "I—I'm not sure," he said. "Maybe what she did wasn't wrong—like illegal."

"Think of it this way," Jeff said. "If she did that same thing to Keiron, how would you feel about it? How would you feel if it was Cynarra?"

Joshua's stomach turned over. It was wrong. The things she had done were wrong.

Slowly, and with great difficulty, he began to write. When a page was done, he would read it to Jeff. Though Joshua's heart burned with shame, Jeff continually reminded him that he was not the one to blame.

He began with his earliest memories, when he was four-years-old and had first gone to live with his aunt.

At one point, he said, "My brothers were there too, sometimes. They—they were pretty rough, too."

"Pretty rough?" Jeff queried.

Joshua bowed his head. "Their physical and sexual abuse began when I was at my aunt's house."

"Do you think your aunt knew about it?" Jeff asked gently.

Joshua sighed. "She knew."

"Just your brothers or other men?"

"Others," Joshua mumbled, wishing the earth would open and swallow him whole.

Jeff waited a moment for him to raise his eyes. "I think that might be what has happened with Keiron."

Joshua groaned. "I won't let him go back," he vowed. "I won't let him ever go back."

"I need to report my suspicions," Jeff said. "I'll talk to Frank later on today."

Joshua nodded. It was the right thing to do. It was what someone should have done for him when he was a little kid.

"Hey, there you guys are!"

Joshua turned at the sound of Missy's voice.

"I can't believe I slept so long. It's almost ten o'clock. And those kids are still sleeping."

"We all had a late night," Jeff said.

Missy glanced down at the notebook in Joshua's hand. He'd closed it as she approached. She must have noticed their serious expressions. She laid a hand on Joshua's shoulder and asked in a gentle voice, "What are you guys doing?"

Jeff didn't answer. Joshua swallowed hard and looked up into his wife's loving eyes. "I'm writing down an account of Yvonne's abuse towards me and the effect it's had on my life."

He didn't know what reaction he'd expected but Joshua was surprised when Missy burst into tears and hugged him. "Oh Joshua," she said, "I'm so proud of you."

As Joshua hugged her back, the feeling he felt most was relief. Why was it that he always somehow still expected condemnation when he told the truth about what had happened?

Missy stood to her feet. "I'll leave you two alone," she said hurriedly. "And I'll keep the kids busy somewhere else. I'll answer the phone. And the door—"

Joshua caught at her hand. He smiled up at her. "We won't let anything interrupt us," he said. "Your father is keeping me on task."

"We'll finish today— or tomorrow for sure," Jeff said.

Missy relaxed a little. "Thanks, Dad," she said softly. She laid a hand on Joshua's shoulder. "You know this is the topic for this week's support group—confronting the abuser."

He had forgotten. There was so much else happening. He hoped they would be able to get together for a support group meeting this week.

"It will be good if you can read your statement for the group," Missy said.

Joshua looked down at the pages of scribbled writing in his hand.

"I'll help you," Jeff said.

Joshua glanced gratefully up at his father-in-law.

"Have you had breakfast yet?" Missy asked.

"Not yet," Jeff said.

"I'll bring it to you," Missy said.

True to her word, Missy deflected all possible interruptions away from Joshua and Jeff. They moved down to Jeff's cabin after Keiron and Cynarra were awake, and continued the painful process of recounting memories.

Missy brought them lunch and shortly after that, Jeff suggested that Joshua take a nap while he went to speak with Frank.

Joshua didn't think he would sleep but he was exhausted physically and emotionally, and he ended up sleeping for almost three hours before Jeff woke him.

Over a pot of coffee, Jeff confessed that he'd also taken some time to visit with Katherine while Joshua had slept. Jamie had sent over some fresh muffins, and Jeff kept the conversation light as they ate. Then it was back to work.

Jeff was a good counselor, reminding Joshua always that he had been just a kid and that it wasn't his fault. Jeff also didn't allow him to minimize or excuse the crimes.

It wasn't until the following day that they began to put it all into one concise statement. Jeff insisted that Joshua write it as a letter to Yvonne.

"Even if she never reads it, this is important for you to do, Josh," he said.

They had included the abuse of his wife and of Cynarra. That had been easier for Joshua to do for some reason. ...Easier to recognize abuse when it was perpetrated upon someone other than himself.

That night he read the statement aloud in front of the support group. It was extremely difficult to do but Joshua knew how important it was, not only for himself but for the six other members of the group.

And then with gentleness and patience, he led each of them to at least begin their own letters of confrontation to their abusers. It was their fourth group meeting, so there was enough trust built between them to allow each other to be honest and open in their sharing time.

They sat around some tables pushed together in the large dining hall.

Jasmine shared first. She had already done a letter. She didn't know the name of the man who had raped her—he'd never been caught—but she said that it had helped her to set down in writing the impact his actions had on her.

Keegan and his brother Lewis had been abused as children, as had Lewis's wife, Starla. Each of them began a letter writing down the life-long effects of that abuse.

Keegan's wife, Randi, had been abandoned physically by her father, and emotionally by her mother. Tears soaked her page as she released her feelings on paper.

And Missy wrote about the impact of Yvonne's words and actions on their lives.

The next day, Missy awoke feeling relaxed and happy. Her morning sickness seemed to have completely passed, and she felt her usual energy and good humor returning.

Missy smiled over at Joshua, still asleep beside her.

She was so thankful to the Lord for all the emotional healing that had occurred in Joshua's life these past few days. And he seemed to be doing better physically as well, with the last of the strep throat infection completely cleared from his system. But he'd still have to take it easy because of his heart condition—no climbing stairs, heavy lifting, and extra stress.

Missy was also thankful that Yvonne had been arrested. She hadn't heard if they'd set a trial date, but she wasn't anxious to think that far ahead yet, anyway.

Keiron was safe. He was legally their foster child now. There was so much healing that needed to happen in that little boy's life as well. Missy and Joshua were determined to provide him a healthy, stable home filled with all the love they had to give.

Missy eased out of bed, careful not to wake Joshua then put on her beautiful silk robe, a gift from her aunt, Coralee, noting with pleasure that it still fit her well enough.

She lingered in front of the mirror, brushing her hair.

"Hey, beautiful…"

Missy turned to see Joshua grinning lazily up at her. She set her brush down and walked over to him.

She bent to kiss him, and Joshua pulled her into a more passionate embrace. Missy melted into his arms…

Suddenly, there was a loud banging that seemed to be coming from just outside their bedroom.

Joshua released her and Missy hurried out of the kitchen and down the narrow hallway that led to the door on the south side of the lodge.

She opened the first door but kept the screen door locked as she saw who it was—Yvonne Quill!

"You're not welcome here," Missy said.

"I want to speak to Joshua."

"Well, you can't."

"That's not for you to say!" Yvonne spat the words angrily at her.

"It is. I'm his wife, and I'm telling you that you are not welcome here."

Yvonne's voice took on a mocking tone. "He has to hide behind his wife's skirts now, does he?"

Red hot anger flared up in her. "Just get out of here, you old witch!"

Missy felt Joshua's hand on her back and his calm voice close to her ear. "It's okay, honey. I'll handle it."

"So there you are," Yvonne smirked. "You gonna let me in or what?"

"No, I'm not," Joshua said.

Yvonne's eyes narrowed and her nostrils flared. "You ungrateful little piece of _____!"

Missy couldn't stop herself. "What has he got to be grateful to you for? Five years of you yelling at him, beating him up, not feeding him properly, not taking him to the hospital when he was sick—"

"It's okay, hon. I got it," Joshua said gently.

Tears sprang to Missy's eyes. "Don't let her in," she pleaded.

"I won't," he said, still speaking in an amazingly calm voice.

"I took care of you when no one else would!" Yvonne yelled. "You were just a dirty, little snot-nosed kid who peed his bed every night."

"The way that you are talking to me now is verbal abuse," Joshua said. "It makes me feel worthless."

"Ha! You are worthless!"

"Your verbal abuse has eroded my confidence. It's made me have difficulty making decisions. All my life—"

Yvonne snorted. "Don't blame me for your problems. You were always a sniveling, whiney little brat. No backbone!"

Missy hadn't noticed Keiron and Cynarra coming up behind them, but Yvonne had.

She curled her lip and pointed her chin. "That one—he's just like you. Whining and crying all the time—"

"Gego!" Joshua yelled.

Missy recognized the Ojibway word as one used in sharp command to a young child. She had even heard people use it to a dog. Loosely, translated, it meant "don't" or "stop!"

Yvonne drew in a sharp breath, turned on her heel and walked away.

Joshua shut the door, leaned back against the wall and then slid down into a sitting position on the floor. He grinned weakly up at Missy then opened his arms towards Cynarra and Keiron. Missy knelt down in front of them to join in a big family, group hug.

And as they rose together to greet the new day, Missy's heart swelled with joy, and a deep gratitude towards her Heavenly Father, the One who had created them and loved them and had promised to be with them forever and ever.

Author's Note

If you have been sexually abused, it is very important that you talk to someone you trust: a teacher or your pastor or youth counselor.

If you know of someone under the age of 14 who is being sexually abused, it is against the law to not report it to the authorities: the police or a social agency.

If you have been sexually abused in the past, the first step on your journey of healing will be to acknowledge that it happened and that it is affecting you today. You need to look honestly at the problems in your life and be willing to accept the help and counsel of others.

To know Jesus is to know the Great Healer. The Bible says that God loves you. He loves you so much that He sent Jesus to pay the price for your sin (it's like somebody taking your jail sentence for you so you can go free). Speaking of Himself in John 10:10 and 11, Jesus said: "I came that they might have life, a great full life. I am the Good Shepherd. The Good Shepherd gives His life for the sheep."

Jesus gave His life for you. But the Good News is that He didn't stay dead. He came alive again after 3 days. The Bible says that He "swallowed up death in victory"! (Isaiah 25:8 and I Corinthians 15:54 KJV).

He only asks us to trust Him. A simple but often difficult decision for someone who has been betrayed by those whom they should have been able to trust. Though your earthly father may have hurt you, your Heavenly Father loves you and because He is perfect, His love for you is perfect.

Life here on earth may be difficult but it is a journey we all must take. There is Someone who wants to walk beside us. When we talk to God and tell Him of our troubles, He hears us and the Bible says that the Holy Spirit is there to comfort us. As you read more of the Bible, you will learn more about God and He will speak truth to your mind and to your heart.

The Lord bless you!

M. Dorene Meyer
dorene@dorenemeyer.com

Recommended Resources

1. The Holy Bible—available in many versions. Find one that's easy for you to read.
2. Visit www.risingabove.ca—excellent site that will direct you towards resources, conferences in your area, and hope and healing.
3. *Hope for the Hurting,* by Howard Jolly, published by Rising Above Counseling Agency in 1996.
4. *How to Counsel a Sexually Abused Person,* by Selma Poulin, also published by Rising Above Counseling Agency.
5. *Helping Victims of Sexual Abuse,* by Lynn Heitritter and Jeanette Vought, published by Bethany House Publishers in 1989.
6. *A Door of Hope,* by Jan Frank, published by Thomas Nelson Publishers in 1993.

Questions for Group Discussion or Personal Reflection—Week Four

Confronting the person who has abused you in the past, or is still abusing you now, may not seem worth all the trouble it will cause. The reason that you may feel this way is low self-esteem, which is a direct result of the abuse! You may even minimize the abuse and its effects because of fear of the confrontation process. Hopefully, by now, you have shared with a counselor and in a support group, and have people around you who will help you to take this important step.

Never enter a situation that may be physically dangerous. If the person you are confronting has a history of physical violence, do not place yourself or others in danger. Leave things to the police; that's their job. Confronting the abuser has proved helpful in the case of recovery from child sexual abuse when the aggressor was a close family member, such as a father or uncle. This step is not intended for cases where the victim is still a child or where there is any possibility of violence (such as spousal abuse).

An advocate is sometimes needed. If the victim is a child or is a person unable to remove themselves from the abuse, there may need to be an advocate. This advocate could be a law enforcement officer or a child protection worker. Their job is to ensure that the person is removed from the abusive situation. Sometimes even adults need someone to advocate for them if the abuse has been ongoing since childhood or if the victim is physically ill or in some other way incapacitated.

Never go alone! If you have been a victim to this aggressor in the past, you may once again be abused if you are alone with that person. God has made us a part of His family. There are people who will care for you and help you through this process. It is preferable that the people who go with you to confront the abuser be trained, professional counselors.

Choose the time and location carefully. It is important that **you** are comfortable and do not feel threatened in the environment that is chosen. It is essential that there be no interruptions and that you have absolute privacy. Children, especially, should be protected from hearing any of the conversation.

Be clear about the proposed agenda and the predetermined goals. Make sure that the agreed-upon purpose for your meeting with the abuser is not "reconciliation." There are no Band-Aid solutions—the wounds are too deep. The stated goal must be to confront the abuser, nothing more. You do not have to extend forgiveness at this time. A later date may be arranged (again with other people present) when this might happen.

Prepare well beforehand. It is important that you are **very** well prepared for any confrontation that will take place. Do not rush this preparation time. You need to write down what you intend to say. This should include:

1. the specific events of abuse
2. the effects that abuse has had on your life

Share this statement with your counselor or support group **before** you confront the abuser. Your counselor will help you with this confrontation process. Often a person who has been abused will continue to blame themselves for the abuse. This is not a time for you to apologize. Think of it as a "victim impact statement" (which is sometimes used in a court of law).

Preparing this "statement" can be useful even if the perpetrator is no longer alive or it is not safe or practical to confront him/her. Writing a letter (unsent) to a former abuser can be an important part of the healing process for some people.

Come prepared with a written statement. You have waited all these years. This is your time. Talk slowly and read what you have written. Those who have come with you to support you should make sure that you are not interrupted. You cannot predict the abuser's response. He/she may be repentant but will more likely be in defensive mode.

Don't expect a quick fix. None of us like to face the reality of our own wrongdoing. We are all masters of denial. The Bible tells us that "the heart is deceitful above all things and desperately wicked; who can know it?" Don't expect that your abuser will readily admit to his sin. His/her first response (as our first response might be) will likely be denial in one form or another.

Don't rush any part of the process. Hopefully, you have allowed two or more hours of uninterrupted time in a private location (no children coming in unexpectedly). Again, no one likes to be confronted with past sin. Don't expect that you will have this opportunity again (i.e.: "we'll talk about this some other time"). Don't be put off. This is your one opportunity.

Pray before you go. If there was ever a time when you need God's help, it is at this moment. One of satan's names is "the deceiver." He is also called: "the father of lies." Pray for the Holy Spirit—the Spirit of Truth—to be present before, during and after your confrontation.

Believe God for a miracle. With God all things are possible. He can heal your wounded heart. He can heal the heart of your abuser. The Bible cautions us to be as gentle as doves and as wise as serpents. Go fully prepared; go with knowledgeable support; and go knowing that even if it seems you have "failed," truth will have been spoken. Allow time for the Spirit of Truth to continue the good work that has begun this day.

A Victor's Song

I have felt recently
That success is near
Just around the corner, just a breath away.

I should be happy
Seeing the mountaintop in view
The reward of a long and difficult climb.

But instead of elation, I know fear
Instead of joy, I feel a dragging hesitation
Making me want to turn and run back to where I began.

Success, that illusive foe
Repels me with its unknown qualities
Failure, like a worn-out coat, wraps around me like a shroud.

Inches from the goal, I turn back
Afraid that someone such as I
Could never, should never, win so grand a prize.

But through the mists
Comes a voice I know so well
Dear child, don't you know? You're already a hero to Me.

You've nothing to prove
It won't matter if you win or lose
My love for you is the same. It will never, ever change.

Run into success!
Don't be afraid of failure.
Rest in My love, child... You're already a hero to Me.

Coming in October

Back to the beginning...

Rachel's Children

—A Novel—

M. D. Meyer

Jenny Wilson, an investigative reporter, finds more than she bargained for: Jeff Peters, the man who mysteriously disappeared from her life three years before; Missy, the child she thought was dead; and a story that could make headlines across the world.

But if Jenny publishes what she knows, Jeff may be sent to prison, Missy could lose her father, and Jenny will have betrayed her new friends.

It is a choice that only she can make.